NIGHTS

Other Books by H.D.

NIGHTS

by **H. D.** [John Helforth]

Introduction by PERDITA SCHAFFNER

A NEW DIRECTIONS BOOK

Copyright © 1986 by Perdita Schaffner

All rights reserved. Except for brief passages quoted in a newspaper, magazine, radio, or television review, no part of this book may be reproduced in any form or by any means, electronic or mechanical, including photocopying and record- ing, or by any information storage and retrieval system, without permission in writing from the Publisher.

Manufactured in the United States of America
Original 100 copies printed by Imprimerie Darantiere, Dijon, France, by friends of the author for private circulation.
First published as New Directions Fine Press Edition, printed by A. Colish in 1986.

LIBRARY OF CONGRESS CATALOGING-IN-PUBLICATION DATA
H. D. (Hilda Doolittle), 1886–1961
  Nights.
  (A New Directions Book)
  I. Title.
PS3507.O726N5 1986   813′.52   85-28472
ISBN 0-8112-0979-2 *(fine press edition)*

New Directions Books are published for James Laughlin by New Directions Publishing Corporation, 80 Eighth Avenue, New York 10011

INTRODUCTION

Who, to begin with, is this John Helforth, one book writer, author of *Nights*? He doesn't exist. He never did. His name is a pseudonym, he is H.D.'s alter ego. He redoubles as the fictitious John, first-person narrator of the prologue. He characterizes himself as a humble wage-earner, an editor of scientific brochures, and a writer manqué. The latter doesn't bother him too much; he has no time to indulge in dubious creative pursuits. Yet—unusual for a man of austere outlook and financial limitations—he has, in the past, managed to undergo a lengthy and costly course of psychoanalysis with the renowned Dr. Frank of Vienna. He used to know a woman called Natalia. A fringe character, he makes clear. Not a friend, more an acquaintance. He never took her seriously, he didn't even like her. He lived in England. She spent most of her time abroad with a strange incestuous retinue—a husband, Neil; a lover, David; and a female half-lover Renne, who was also her sister-in-law, and who was, in turn, captivated by a famous international actress, Una. Natalia was a frustrated writer. Her work was as undisciplined as her life, brilliant, but lacking focus. Neither one thing nor another, neither popular nor genuinely esoteric. Fragmentary, over-wrought, and overwritten; self-indulgent, a blind-ing reflection of her own exasperating ego. She dreamed up a mathematical formula as the answer to her problems. "Two straight lines run into in-finity." She proved it by skating into an ice hole in a mountain lake.

"She left her watch on the muff," said Renne, reporting the details of the suicide. "My watch," she added.

Stylish to the end.

She also left a novel entitled *Nights*. Renne per-suaded John to read it and to write an introduction —which he did, and which we have here. The dif-ficult unpublishable novel follows.

Natalia, Renne, Neil. They were all real people. But, John elucidates, those were not their real names. He has taken them from the book's protago-nists, whom we now encounter. A twist, an unusual gimmick. Fiction superimposed on fiction, boxes within boxes, trompe l'oeil, mirror tricks. The pragmatic John looking on, looking in from the sidelines of the introduction, seeing right through Natalia's perfervid idiosyncrasies. And the book itself with the very flaws and excesses he has just criticized.

These devices permit H.D. to write exactly as she pleases while sternly evaluating herself. I suspect she had a lot of fun—and some pain—exploring these different dimensions. The prose sparkles. The love scenes are startlingly explicit. And if it is all rather high flown, and cryptic and elliptical at times . . . well, that's just what John was complaining about.

She is, once again, writing of what she knows. But not with the claustrophobic immediacy of *Bid Me to Live*—which was essentially a transcript; or the emotional stream of consciousness of *HERmione*; or the nostalgia, historical legend, and supernatural overtones of *The Gift*.

Natalia's absence through death and John's restraining presence create, between them, a framework imposing restrictions which, paradoxically, free her invention. The characters are totally recognizable to anyone of her immediate circle—as I was at the time. She has switched them around, however, and changed their motivations.

The Natalia of the introduction and of the ensuing tale is, of course, H.D. herself—multifaceted, every nerve exposed.

Renne is Bryher, her lifelong companion, recast as husband Neil's sister. She is didactic and bossy, running everybody's life without being fully in charge of her own, quoting and misquoting Freudian profundities. And very wealthy. Natalia's marriage was a haphazard arrangement, something she drifted into, a matter of propinquity and expediency. "Here we all are," they might have said, "we don't know where we're going, let's try this out and see what happens." Give Kenneth Macpherson a twist—the charismatic younger man whom H.D. loved deeply, whom Bryher appropriated as a husband; a marriage of convenience which kept the family together in an outwardly respectable manner.

In the narrative Neil has taken off for Italy and a gay life style as it would now be termed. So it was with Kenneth, but he followed his new orientation to the South of France.

Neil never appears directly on stage, or rather, I should say, on camera. My family was into film-making at that time, and it shows. H.D. has reversed the process—and also carried it a stage further —pretending the book is really a film. Her technique is cinematic, a restless dizzying montage. It darts and zooms, pans in on tantalizing close-ups, veers off again, highlights vignettes in lost corners. Most of it at one remove—exposition, recollection. The only characters we really meet are Natalia and her new lover David. Their bed is the epicenter. He starts out as a bit of a clod, nonintellectual, very very English. As the characterization grows, he becomes more and more like Neil. There, her invention has faltered. David is a composite, not a very successful one. A number of young men did pay court— admirers, disciples, lovers maybe, maybe not. None of them lasted or meant much to her. After Kenneth, nobody could.

Natalia lives in considerable comfort, attended to by a busybody housekeeper and the chauffeur who drives her to the death tryst on the frozen lake. Renne's house, and her concept, maintained with her money. A modern house, all concrete and glass; straight lines, flat surfaces, sharp angles; set high on a rocky base. Natalia claims to love it. She idealizes its geometric quality. In actual fact, H.D. was never fully at home in Kenwin, the Bauhaus Kenneth and Bryher devised as a film studio. She—as did I— found it cold, both in temperature and spirit. And fraught with personality clashes. The architecture acted as an echo chamber for arguments.

We were terribly ingrown, a volatile microcosm in the vastness. I was caught up in it, and trapped, yet an outsider, a gawky adolescent without a clue as to what was going on. I missed a lot, but I will never forget the tensions. Luckily, there was sur-cease from time to time. Visitors broke the intensity. They stayed at nearby hotels, never in the house it-self. Their arrival was discussed for weeks, dreaded as an intrusion, yet longed for as a distraction—especially by me. Disciplined and overscheduled as they were, some turned up impulsively, checked into their hostelry, telephoned later.

"It's Elisabeth!"

What could have happened, what did she want now? She was supposed to be filming at Elstree Studios, and discussing a play with a London pro-ducer. Dear me, how very difficult. Bryher would go into an absolute spin, beside herself with secret euphoria like a schoolgirl in the throes of a new crush. That's about the way it was. Elisabeth Berg-ner, then at the peak of her career. Bryher didn't care about glamor and fame, but she was enthralled by the personality, the diminutive mercurial waif with huge brown eyes and lilting Viennese speech. "Bry-y-her, it is so hard, I am so ti-i-red, help me dear Bry-y-her, nobody understands as you do." She was Garbolike in her attitude to fans and crowds, mistrustful of men in power—all men in those days —producers and directors and agents, and her hus-band who was all three. She also adored her station in life. Acting was in her soul, on stage and off.

Kenneth and Bryher had once been called in for help with the translation of a movie script. From then on, Bryher was the only one who understood. A capricious dependency set in, a new half love. It irked H.D. but she went along with it because it gave Bryher an outlet.

Una in *Nights*, Bergner to the life—now we see her, now we don't.

An odd lot, we might well conclude. Jumpy mixed up people with their bisexual conflicts, their wars of nerves, and their forays into the occult—Tarot cards, the two lines to infinity, the haunted Lac de Brey. They take themselves so seriously. They never laugh. Self indulgent as they are, they don't seem to find any joy in their flights of fancy.

Mercifully, H.D. laughed a great deal. Humor was her safety valve. It gave élan to her conversation. She had a beautiful sense of the absurd, a quick wit and turn of phrase. She enjoyed the lighter aspects of life. She needed them. Afternoons at the movies, followed by "a greedy tea" as she called it. She loved to gossip. She had, and was, fun.

Motoring was another favored diversion. We would set off in the stately black Packard, the chauffeur Jules at the wheel, Bryher at his side, the rest of us in back. "Let's go to the Lac de Brey," my mother would exclaim, "it's always different."

She usually won the vote. It was an attractive excursion, about an hour away, up a wild series of hairpin bends, along a grassy plateau, and suddenly we were upon it. Yes, always different, reflecting white peaks or green ones according to the season; golden with sun or black with cloud, sometimes whipped by stiff breezes, other times still and crystalline, or frozen solid. The waters were icy, even in midsummer. And lifeless; no boats, no swimmers, ever. That treacherous current and the bottomless depth, they said—whoever "they" might be, purveyors of folklore from long ago.

It was impossible to know what my mother was thinking behind her dark glasses. She may well have fantasized about taking off and ending it all in a quick swoop. Yet I doubt it. She had a zest for life which Natalia lacked. "Come on now," she would have said, no matter what her mood, "it's time for a greedy tea."

Perdita Schaffner

NIGHTS

Part I: Prologue

I can not do better than use the names in this manuscript, as Natalia Saunderson used them. Her name is not Natalia nor Saunderson, neither is her sister-in-law called Renne, nor her husband, Neil. The last two are living, Natalie is dead.

I knew them all slightly, Neil better than the others, and I do not think, as some of his fervid worshippers do, that Natalia did herself in, to spite him. I don't think there was any spite about it. Neil doesn't think so either. I know Neil really loved her but as the simple word "love" nowadays, needs such lucid volumes of emendations, to be, in any particular case, even recognizable, I hesitate to use it. Renne might have blamed herself, but, I think, Renne was too sensible for that. I don't think any blame was meant to rest anywhere, perhaps if, with anyone, it was with herself; the only untidy thing about her going, was the shelf of manuscripts she left. She was aware that this might prove awkward. She had written, some weeks before her death, a careful series of directions to Renne Saunderson, always beginning and ending each manuscript with a slogan, slightly savouring of Saint Paul, "but better burn." She was too conscientious an artist, herself, to make a bonfire of the lot; or, it might be argued that she was too cowardly. But no—she could kill herself but not the spirit in her. She wrote feverishly, in all sorts of places, fervid stream-of-consciousness (I believe they call it) prose. She jabbed, with an angry pencil, in the margin of one study, "but it's more like music." Her pencil ran away with her; if she stopped writing, she was numb. Sometimes, she stopped long enough to wonder, where it was all taking her. Against one thing she was definite, that was Renne and her perfectly laudable and commendable desire to get her to a nerve specialist. She would hear nothing of Renne's arguments of "inhibition" and "repression." She was the first to shout, "repression—you flatter me, Renne." But evidently, for all her erotic experiments, she could not make an equation that answered, only that last one, *two parallel lines meet.*

They were very straight lines, Renne tells me. It was their chauffeur, Georges Crox, who explained,

4

with the acumen of his kind, that Madame had scuffled a little with her skates; the powdered snow on the ice, showed every gesture of the take-off; the finish was, as if it were, cut by diamond, on glass. The two lines ran straight out, two parallel lines— they met in a dark gash of the luminous ice-surface. She had demonstrated perfectly.

"It was like her to go there," Renne remarked. Renne Saunderson had brought the manuscripts to my office. I told her, beforehand, that I was sure they would be of no practical value to my firm. I had to be clear about that. But Renne said it wasn't actually a matter of the firm publishing the papers; she wanted an introduction from me. From me, of all people! Well, Renne had thought it out, "you see, John," she explained, "you are a half-and-half sort of person yourself." I knew perfectly what she meant by that. My psychological investigations were marred by my own imagination, and when I wanted to let go and write a purely popular, or even slightly acceptable tale or novel, my scientific training spoiled it. I hadn't found the medium to suit me, and hadn't the time, anyway, on my hands, as Natalie, for instance, had, for constant prose experiments. I was earning my own living and only just doing it at that; reader, travelling-salesman and general under-paid, overworked utility-man,

to a publishing firm of semi-popular scientific brochures, hasn't much time, it need hardly be stated,
for other than the most occasional and incoherent
spurts of creative writing. "Of course, I know the
stuff won't do for your publishers," Renne told me,
"but I thought you might tell me, why it won't do
for any."

2

"It won't be difficult to do that," I told Renne.
I knew enough about Natalie, to know that her
problems would have been my problems, but for my
somewhat tantalising scientific habits. I had lost
much and gained little, perhaps, in my explorations
into the new doctrines of the unconscious, neverthe-
less, I had dragged up, from that soul depth, the one
pearl of price, the answer. The answer, it may be
argued, didn't make me any happier, but then, it
might equally be argued, I was as happy as those
who had had no answer. Witness, I might, at this
moment, exclaim, Natalia.

But I don't want to bring up Natalia, as a witness
in this case. She drove two straight lines to infinity
and she got her answer. She did get her answer.
Where I had the stimulating yet painful experience

of psycho-analysis, (those hours I spent with Dr. Frank in Vienna), she had those perilous hours of fervid, analytic concentration on her papers, and in the end—what? I might say, yes; maybe I, also, would prefer not to live, yet ultimate curiosity finds most things fascinating and one, also, wants to see what's round the corner. Also, I promise myself that, one day, I may be rich enough to write a sort of second-rate best seller. Natalia drew the line at the second-rate, she would have the peak or nothing. Well, she had the peak and—nothing.

I feel, she held on to Neil and to Renne's friendship in the hope that it would save her—"it," that is, their friendship, in its various dimensions, not the very human Neil and Renne. She forgot how human Neil was, how faithful yet how erratic Renne. Renne was erratic but Renne was never anything but loyal. I think Neil tired out. He needed something to off-set his own icy hallucinations, and Nat was the last person, really, in the world for him. Maybe, they melted together, in the south, those first years, maybe Neil was trying to escape Neil when he tried to escape Natalia. Nat found the one way to help him.

Renne had stated, as preliminary to our interview about the papers, that it was like Natalia to go there. I did not ask immediately why, nor where.

Later, Renne came out with a story; the scene was as livid and unreal as any jerry-built film set. There was a small lake on the upper plateau, "upstairs" they called it, she told me, on the road between Arignon and Laugy, on the way to some local pub, or other, called, I believe, The Three Crowns. The lac de Brey, that looked so fairy-like and blatantly artificial, set just there, where the road turns through a pine-forest, was anything but artificial, anything but fairy-like, unless you call a depth that is incalculable, "artificial" and the very and exact entrance to inferno, "fairy-like"; I mean, the lac de Brey, Renne explained it, has geographically or geologically, exactly no known depth. It just goes down forever. No plumb-line anyhow, had ever touched it, or the sort of things they measure lakes with, been able to cope with it. A hidden river cut through, from a still higher range, and anything flung in there was not found. Or anyone. "I mean," Renne explained, "we used to think it was a fake or a sort of legend. If nobody ever drowned there, how could you tell that the body would never rise and never be found anywhere along the shores of the larger, lower lake, or even further seaward?" "Did anybody ever drown there?" "Well, not in the memory of man," Renne had emendated. "Did," I questioned, in a manner vaguely reminiscent, to myself, of Frank of Vienna, "people, maybe, not want to be found?" That had not occurred to Renne. "You mean that the place was haunted?" "O, not that," I hastily assured her. "No. But there was some un-plumbed depth in Nat, that surely she was afraid to look for. She didn't look down, inside." "No," said Renne, "that was the trouble. She always made us look up."

That was just it. Renne put her finger on it. Natalia was like that princess in a tale who had to climb a mountain, a glass-mountain at that. I don't remember the story, only the illustration in our nursery-Grimm, of a princess placing spike on spike in the smooth surface of a conventionally peaked, illustration mountain, while she made a ladder of it, then climbed these rungs, one after one, to—where? I have forgotten. Well, anyway it seemed to me, Natalie was like that. I had known her only slightly, in the beginning, and there is no use dragging up her whole past, as an introduction to her would-have-been present. She never got away from that past, she went on repeating that past, as we all do—well, not all. Renne and I could look at each other, both with a secret, grim sort of satisfaction. We have "resolved" our problem, definitely and scientifically —for what it is worth.

If Natalia had resolved her problem, she wouldn't

have gone on writing. But the tragedy of it is, she didn't get any fun out of her writing, any more than we may have been said to have got any fun out of our separate infernos or inquisitions of analysis. But Natalia made a gesture. Renne and I, grim and philosophical, were too wise to do that. Neil was too indifferent. Only Natalia had the courage to cut two straight lines, on a flat surface of an Alpine lake, running to infinity. Infinity? I think, she found that.

3

She would have been glad to know, but we can't tell her, that Neil missed her. Of course she knew from the first, just what she was doing; in the words of the excellent Crox, "Madame prevailed nicely." Not that it needed much argument to persuade him to go on to the Trois Couronnes, and have a smoke and get warm. She wanted to do the "round" of the lake, he had explained, sensible of his position. He would be loyal, as loyal as was permitted, to Madame. She had added another legend to their lake. Also, it was "logic," Madame might do that, as did not Mademoiselle herself remember, how often they three, or they two, or even one of them, used to get out? Or, in the pays d'Enhaut, or, in the valley? Yes, of course, Renne remembered.

She might have been happier, not to have been able to visualise, as she told me, each tiny act of Natalia Saunderson, her brother's wife. First, Nat would lean forward, be conversational, it was colder up here. Crox would reply that it was still colder en haut, but the snow was descending nicely. Here, already there was powder on the trees. And ah, the lake is frozen, she would exclaim as they rounded the bend. That sâle lac, he would mutter, as he had so often muttered; he was able to abuse it; it was all in the family, Natalia knew that quite well. But O, it is so beautiful. You find it? He wanted her to go on telling him about the lake, the beauty of the sparsely wooded, moss-covered slopes. And last summer—But Madame was wise not to go out with young Monsieur David, in the row-boat. She agreed; he was often careless. And that lake, Madame, he repeated, is sans fond.

She might even have listened to his legend of the lake. She had heard it before. Then, as if on the spur of the moment, "I think I'll get out," she would say. There was an old muff, a cross between a foot-stool and a lap-rug that they called "Aemilia," nobody knew why. Neil said, "why yes, it's the one, you remember, of our Aunt Aemilia." But

Renne said, that that wasn't why they called the muff, Aemilia. "I think, I'll take Aemilia," Natalia might say, as if as an after-thought. All of them, including Crox (who may have wondered why les Anglaises referred to a muff, by the name of his late grandmother) called the muff, "Aemilia." Nat had known, all along, that she would take Aemilia. Her skates were stuffed neatly inside.

"So Madame took the muff, Mademoiselle. How was I to know she would have her skates inside it?"

4

"Those damn skates," we all might have said, but can anything be quite damned that is the instrument of one who makes, once in its existence, one perfect gesture? She laid the muff down on the near bank. Crox could barely have got out of sight; she didn't make a dramatic turn of the lake or stagger, half-frozen, to an opposite bank, to make an effective exit; she did it right there. She might have argued that she would lose her nerve if she made the turn, under the dwarf saplings, to the other side, where she had first stopped with her husband, to note some effect of broken light and shadow, thrown from tall, frozen grasses, on the clear ice.

She might have argued, "there Neil took the photograph, and the memory of those days will break
me," or, equally, she might have reasoned, that on
this near bank, she might be stopped by any stray
motor or a passing farm-cart. But I don't suppose,
she stopped to think of anything. She went straight
to the nearest convenient point, for this final take-
off. She knew perfectly, that once on the clear ice,
nothing could ever stop her.

She probably sat on the wide muff, to strap on her
skates; the powdered snow lay undisturbed about
it. She made the necessary, preliminary "skuffle,"
to translate Crox from the vernacular, and was off.
She got her footing; she swung out like a Nordic
skating champion on a news-reel. The lake was,
maybe, half a mile across, maybe, a mile and a half
long. She did not pass its centre, for the world
knows that no one ever skates on the lac de Brey.
There is one boat-house, and water-lilies star the
edge in summer. She may have remembered that she
and David had come here, that summer (was it last
summer), anyhow, when Neil had gone off to—to—
she would forget that Neil had gone off anywhere
or with anybody. She might wonder, for a moment,
if she had done well. After all, Renne had trusted
her, she was to join a group of their friends out
from London, at Lausanne; that League crowd were

doing their usual winter dramatist sort of charade, they called a play, for charity. Nat had even, half-promised, she might have remembered, to be one of the official programme sellers. O, what is it she remembered?

I do not visualise her skirt swirling and whirling, like that ice-Pavlova—we all know her from our news-reel—or her arms, at the last, flung out, in a dramatic gesture. I see her upright, swaying, swinging out. She was nothing. A sort of pencil. She was upright, and "we suppose," said Renne, "that she had on her mole-cap, it was the one missing." She would wear a small, mole-skin cap, pulled over her ears. "She left her watch on the muff."

"What," I remember at last, shouting at Renne—all this was in my office—"do you mean?" It seemed, at last, that I had reached a limit. I knew all about Natalia Saunderson. She didn't get any publicity; the season that year was rich in accidents. There had been the usual broken rope and the usual English climbers who had gone over the usual, fashionable, Engadine ridge; people were tired of "accidents" and anyhow, this lake and this particular corner of the world were never fashionable. Neither was Nat Saunderson. She had disappeared, she re-appeared, she wrote, she published, but it was, none of it, satisfactory. "O, she's always abroad, why doesn't she stay in England?" Or, "O, it's that tiresome group she's with now." Or, "O, this," or "O, that." But a Sunday edition did manage to feature an early photograph, inset in a news-reel corner of (of course) the wrong lake. It was Renne who sent me that cutting, before I heard the story.

"She left her watch on the muff." I asked Renne to repeat the statement. It sounded like a mid-Victorian French grammar, gone demented. "Her what?" "Her watch. Or rather," Renne added, "it was my watch."

5

It is this sort of thing that makes life unbearable. I had to fortify myself with the lingo of our counting house, Renne's and mine, fortify myself with, or try to fortify myself with, the language of the unconscious. It had hit me, square in the nose. I had been so neatly guarded. Nat Saunderson was erratic, had had a husband, had had a lover, had managed a divorce somehow, had finally married Neil and everyone said, that's that, and, in their several capacities, washed their hands of Nat Saunderson and her problems. For myself, I never took her seriously—I said to myself, I never took her seriously, and didn't really like her. But when Renne made up her astonishing sentence, out of an out-worn French grammar of the Victorian era, I was un-done.

The idea of the watch on the muff, upset me.

I tried to convey to Renne that I was vaguely amused and I gave a sort of chortle.

It was the chortle we all give in the face of the unknown, a cross between a crow and a jeer, to show that we aren't frightened.

And anyhow, why should I be frightened?

It would be an interesting incident, a little some-thing to proffer Professor Frank, should I ever find time for another series of séances with him, in Vienna. Frank? Vienna?

But I had resolved my problems, I was busy. I wanted to write. We can't bother Frank of Vienna with all these little nothings. But damn Nat Saunderson.

It was the sort of thing she would do.

"I suppose, at the last, she jerked out her sleeve, the way she did—" "Yes, to see what time it was." "Why should she want—" But Renne did not finish the sentence that I left hovering. Why indeed should she want to know what time it was? It was one of the indefinite afternoon hours, I supposed. They would have had lunch, she and the housekeeper,

Renne always left at Les Murs; the housekeeper would be told not to wait tea. Why, I could even see that now, hear her words, "Fräulein Hart-mann—" the housekeeper was from Zürich—"don't wait tea, if I'm late." I wondered what language she spoke, Nat was teaching the Hartmann English and they talked a sort of pig-French between them, as a compromise, Nat was shy of German. I, who seemed to know so little, who had spent only those odd week-ends with them at Les Murs, on the way to or from Vienna or, in the old days, on my rare vacation trips to Italy, yet knew all that. I knew, really, everything.

I said, "she would, of course, tell the Hartmann not to wait tea. Then she would—she would—" Renne said, "yes, one seemed to know everything, she would do. But one would never have known, (would one) she would do that?" By that, of course, she meant, the watch on the muff.

6

Renne jerked out her arm. She did not have to tell me. That was the watch. Renne withdrew her wrist, as quickly. I understood what Renne did not say, "at the last, she was thinking of us." It was an obligation, the smallest possible obligation, but that made it so much worse. Nat had borrowed a watch. She was returning a watch. She had her own, of course. Renne did say, as she turned to leave me, "though the others laugh, John, you and I know." By that, she meant, though the others scoff at us and our attempt to readjust, through the much mis-understood medium of psycho-analysis, we know just what that gesture, on the part of a woman who premeditated death, meant. It meant somehow, in the fabulous heiroglyph of the Freudian tech-nology, that she preferred Renne and her affinities to her own. ("She had her own watch. She wore mine. Mine was being regulated at Lausanne. I asked Nat to bring it, when she came." This, from a letter afterwards. Renne knew I knew, but for her own sake, she desired to be explicit.) Nat had left a wristwatch. Nat had always by her, two watches (she was fantastically punctual) yet, as she was leaving Les Murs, for the last time, automatically or deliberately strapped Renne's watch round her wrist. She wanted to be Renne, she would rather have been Neil's sister.

This may seem to the layman, too obvious or not obvious enough. To me, it is quite clear. Nat loved Neil and he, her. But there was a catch about it. There is no use going into the technology of the "incest barrier." She loved Neil Saunderson. They were lovers; that love broke. Neil ricocheted off into another layer. He loved or thought he loved these young men. He wanted to escape Nat. Renne stood between them. Renne would have saved her, saved Neil. Renne later saved Neil. But, at what sacrifice.

7

A small, mannish platinum or platinum-plated watch, with a wide strap, was left on a strip of dark fur, by the side of a small lake, on the edge of the road leading from Arignon to the plateau, above Laugy. The chauffeur picked it up, and saw that it was going. "It was," Renne told me, he told her, "just half past three, exactly." He had not given Renne time to walk round the lake. Usually, on these occasions, he allowed just one hour. That day he had barely stayed twenty minutes, at the Couronnes. He too had a "tic" about time, and he and Renne would often compare their watches. His first thought was that she had been attacked, robbed maybe. There had been an outbreak of crime due to the general unrest in Europe and the rigours of the chô-mage, lately, in various quarters. He saw then, in an instant. "I knew, Mademoiselle, what had hap-

pened." With the fidelity of his kind, he waited, as
a dog may wait beside a swiftly running river, after
a boat has capsized, though he knew it was no use.
No one passed. His primitive tact forbade him to
leave the spot. He felt the spirit would rest there,
was still hovering over the sheet of pure ice, under,
far under which, the body floated. The body, he
visualised (the legend of this lake was familiar,
from his boyhood) might be still whirling down-
ward. No plumb-line nor any of the new-fangled
devices for measuring depth of water, had ever here,
struck bedrock. Or it might have reached the end,
and have been caught in a counter-current. It was
known that this lake was the overflow from some
hidden river. He could think like that, for he was
French, he was Vaud, he was logical, he was sane,
he was mad. "Les Anglais sont fous," he said under
his breath, for the thousandth time or the millionth,
in his life. Here was another instance of their folly.

8

I would be glad if I could dismiss Nat Saunderson
with a logic as brutal. No doubt Georges Crox had
inherited from centuries of mountain-dwelling pre-

decessors, just that attitude. He had to be defensive; if he had not learnt, in childhood, just that power of repudiation, before the mysteries of nature, he himself would have gone mad. There was no family, really, of his acquaintance, who had not some furtive secret, some almost legendary, idiot, their toll to that nature that left them protected, yet insulated. Madness, as is well known, runs in those secluded districts. Perhaps Nat *was* mad. Perhaps the mountains got her and their spirit. This is the catch.

If Nat herself, say, some two years ago or even a year ago, had brought me these very pages, I should have had some idea of how to deal with them. I would have looked on Natalia Saunderson as a woman with a gift, an unquestionable talent. I would not have questioned her gift, but would have suggested a complete re-casting of her whole theme, to make it, not so much saleable, as merely presentable. I would not, actually, have criticised her manner of presentation, (I find in certain phrases, an indescribable perfection of sheer presentation) but the matter! Not that people do not write of love, of crosscurrents of lovers, husbands, what-not. It wasn't that with Natalia Saunderson. Every line seemed to bleed fire. Or ice. Ice and fire, I suppose, exactly. The reasoning, the presentation of the emotional situation, is true, that is the catch, too terribly, too blazingly true, to be quite bearable. If I, who could follow the intricacy and daring of the sheer technique of her writing, found it impossible, how could she ever hope to reach, not the ordinary common-or-garden reader (that obviously was out of the question), but even the more or less affable intellectual? Her battery was surcharged. She was presenting truth, or what she saw as truth, in other words, not as a photographer, a journalist, or even a portrait-painter or a dramatist, but in some other medium. She seemed to work actually in radium or electricity. Is that, I ask you, the medium for a novel? I could name you a half-dozen, living, skilled novelists, far more capable of presenting life and its minutae, than Natalia Saunderson. Nor do I speak of poetry. Poetry after all, solves its own problem. There, emotion, no matter how true, how brutally realistic, can be translated into another symbol, a sort of hieroglyph of rhythm and metre and poetical image. We say, "that is poetry," it can be labelled poetry, "O, it is only poetry." Prose, too, is another question. The tactful novelist can nowadays, there is no question of it, say almost anything he wants. He must be careful about it, however, and a little bit false; in other words, from time to time, he must, for his own sake, for the sake of his public, not to mention his publisher, definitely, have his tongue in his cheek. That sort of novel gets across—well, Natalia did not have her tongue in her cheek.

There is something definitely and indecently true about these pages, that she calls "Nights." She evidently wrote them one after another, following, if I may hazard a guess, the actual experience. If I may use my power of psycho-analytic dissection or even vivisection, I would say, that she had actually gone to David Leavenworth's room, as she describes it in these pages, at Les Murs. That she had wanted a relationship with him, in order to counteract her bitter sense of the loss of Neil, her husband. I do not say, this is any excuse. There was, it may be argued, no excuse whatever. The David of the story, she has made it quite clear, was a young man, a visitor, almost a total stranger. He had known Neil, she had outlined her story to him. Renne might have been helpful, she indicates, but Renne is occupied with a half-relationship with some fascinating actress who is apparently staying in the neighbourhood. I could corroborate all this, get the actual facts from Renne Saunderson, but I don't know that I want to. Unusual writing nowadays has insuperable barriers. A person like Nat, with no practical idea of values, with no ghost of a shadow of talent for the "false," that is so necessary for presentation, has no chance. She becomes merely an automatic recorder of the

social life around her, in other words, a sort of supe-
rior society gossip, or she becomes the thing that is
really irreconcilable, a sort of scientific lyrist. What
do I mean? I mean, I think, just that.

The actual facts are actual facts, she almost dem-
onstrates them on a blackboard. But to what heights
she lifts us through all the exposition of her furtive
visits to the bedroom of a visitor in the house of her
sister-in-law, Renne Saunderson. There is no vulgarity about it. Alas, if there only had been. Isn't
vulgarity a requisite of sheer life? If only she could
have twisted it all sideways, padded it out, pre-
sented a moral, made a "happy ending," all might
have been well. The trouble with Nat Saunderson
was, that she wouldn't project herself, materialise
herself, for any sort of public.

9

She couldn't present herself even for the very
small public that was hers, undoubtedly, Renne and
Neil Saunderson. Apparently, she said nothing to
them about it. I don't exactly mean about her liason
with David Leavenworth, but about the reasons she
may have had for proving something that she had

already proved, that love, of any sort, casual or otherwise, in its normal physical aspect, wasn't for her. It was, as if for the last time, she had perfectly demonstrated that with Neil, whom she loved actually. As a child, I was set to trace black lines, round a half-familiar map to memorize it. So she. She seemed to take a pencil and run it round the contour of a psychic map, demonstrating and repeating something. It was as if she said, I know this is true, I know it is no good, but look at me, I am doing it. Why should she have wanted us to look at her? I don't suppose she did, really. I imagine that she found there was something wanting, she couldn't face that on top of Neil's desertion (that psychic desertion, I suppose, was what had maimed her) and so she dallied with a pencil, maybe, in bed in her own room, with a night-light, by her, on the table. Surely—here enters the moralists, in the person of John Helforth—she would not have bothered with these notes, if she had been happy, and the only excuse for that sort of thing, if nowadays excuse is necessary, is happiness. If she had been "happy," even if she had been vaguely "comforted," would she, I ask you, have rushed, after each visit of David Leavenworth to her room, or her visits to his room, to a pad and pencil, to jot down the experience? Happiness is "my cup runneth over."

25

Her cup did not run over. It was empty. She had emptied it with Neil's going and she knew very well there could be no "other." But there was the crystal goblet, someone surely must see that there was a goblet, even if it was empty. I suppose the Leaven-worth of her story (I have no idea who he may be, and don't want to know) supplied something. She speaks of his magnetism, as if he were an animal.

10

Her writing did not satisfy her, it was too lumin-ous, too cerebral altogether. To be honest, if she had brought this manuscript to me herself, if the living Nat Saunderson, in her tailored town-costume and her slightly a-symmetrical eyebrows, had laid it on my office table, as later her sister-in-law, Renne did, I don't believe I would have been specially impressed at first glance. On mature consideration, I should have been entirely won over and extravagantly en-thusiastic with the method of her writing, but frankly, as I have already said, the subject would have shocked me. Not the actual visits to anybody's actual bedroom, but the blatant lightning-realism. Realism of the dust-on-the-commode school wasn't for her. She wanted the realism of white lightning, of the "radium ray" she spoke of. She wanted truth of that order, and she was not the first to want it. There was another dame, burnt to ashes, Semele, I think her name was and a boy, driving his father's chariot. Also, countless tales in history, of the stealers-of-fire order, men who for man, would drag down fire from heaven. She certainly seemed competent to do it, judging her by her uncompromising frankness.

"Look here," I might have said, "this is good stuff. But it needs a little padding."

I might have said that.

"Have a cigarette?" I might have said, after reconsidering her pages, "I read the stuff again last night, sitting up in bed. You do make that scene live."

I might have said that.

"Look here, Natalia, this is a sort of sketch for a play. Here you have everything but—"

"Ah, but?" she might have asked me, and, in my thought, I shiver at that a-symmetrical frown as she draws (in my imagination) her brows together, as if in order to understand something utterly too base to be proffered to her consideration. I don't know why I feel a worm, when I think of Natalia and of what I might have said, what fortunately (or alas, unfortunately) I never did say.

11

And yet I'm left to say it, trust Renne. Why didn't Renne, herself, get down to it, tackle this difficult piece of writing? I asked Renne. "I am too near," she said simply and there was nothing, there never had been, that one could ever say to contradict Renne Saunderson, when she made a simple state-ment. It was like the Delphic oracle. "Well—get some—get some competent chap to do it." Renne didn't say anything. I thought, "she's thinking, 'there ain't no sich person'." But I contradicted, in thought, my thought. Renne could never, possibly, have expressed herself in the vulgar Dickens' idiom.

"There is nothing to be done about it," I finally told Renne Saunderson, "but to accept or destroy the pages."

12

Here are the pages. Night I, Night II, Night III, set out in their order, as in the original, not too untidy manuscript. I am enough of a writer to know, that Nat wrote them straight off, without thinking and without re-touching. I am enough of a psychol-ogist to guess that she was defending herself or trying to convince herself that something was worth doing, that she knew wasn't.

Also, she had to choose definitely between the sugar-coated "happy ending" school of writing, and the back to the pig-sty erotic realism. As I have said, with tact, you can present almost anything, under one or the other formula. She chose neither.

Her skates on the lac de Brey, that winter after-noon, made a simple statement. It was a mathemati-cally simple statement. So with these pages. She had put down something that happened and as it hap-pened. The catch is, that it doesn't read as if it ever happened, because such things don't happen to other people or if they happen, I am sure, they don't hap-pen like that. But, then, neither would anyone else, I am sure, have chosen that particular lake on that particular plateau, on the road between Arignon and Laugy, on the way to the Trois Couronnes, for an exit. And neither would anyone else, I am sure, have spoiled such an utterly concentrated and beautifully abstract gesture, by leaving (God help us all) some-body's borrowed watch, at the last, on an old muff.

Part II: Nights

NIGHT I

Natalia, they had called her; but it was Nat or Neith now. Neit or Neith is what he called her; he said, "Neith" and she felt rhymes go with the word; sheathe, unsheathe—claws certainly. He says, "you have no need to be so cruel. You bully me." He says, "it was cruel."

He repeats, "it was cruel," but she is too grateful for the magnetic over-sensuality of his mouth to speak. He will spoil it, of course; he is too young to know how important it is. He will, of course, force her out of her trance, renew her in an old mould. The old mould does not fit. He does not know how important it is for her to realise this. She manages, "don't talk about what we did. I told you it was the beauty of splintered ice; on top of the ice, I told you, he is like that, and you make it possible for me to endure living with them this way." He says, "thank

God," and she is afraid, he will try to mould himself to a dramatic unit. He will not know how great he is and she will have to force herself to sit up. He will not know what he gives her, unless she tells him.

She thinks: there is an awful reality about this. I wonder if I will ever be able to get away, once having committed myself. No one ever kissed me like that, into blackness. Blackness rises up. That is, because his mouth closes over mine, like that. I can't breathe. Neith—breathe. I am Nat or Natalia or Neith, as they now call me. I am really not as important as all that; Neith is in the Luxor temple. I am negated, blotted out by Neil's incredible unfaithfulness. Women live only on their self-esteem; I am blotted out but not dead. This kiss and no breathing— breathe, Neith—will kill me, then I am dead. I never thought that I could take another lover. This boy is young enough to be woman or child. He adores me. How much does he know, anyway? His kiss, after all, is old, incredibly mature, sleep and opiate.

She shook off opiate; her voice raised into ordinary dimension. She heard her voice, modulated, but not whispering: "listen, get this clear." The words were terse, purposely timed, she listened to appraisement and judgment, that meant nothing, "you know I have been faithful." He said, "you needn't be so cruel. You needn't start to bully me again, like that."

She said, "I only want you to know—I love Neil."
This meant nothing.

"He is young enough, he is child enough," she kept
saying, to get over her own black-phobia of ap-
proaching guilt. But why should I feel, guilty? She
did not know whether it was worse that Neil loved
this boy of his or whether it would have left her
completely disintegrated and hence "free," if he had
loved a woman. Neil's lovers were like that; they
were intolerably, their children. But she did not
want a child, nor Neil, nor would she risk the silver
and Brazilian-blue of their love by casual pin-stab
of the new psychology. Renne, with her usual, intolerable logic, said, "what you and Neil both need
is a good stiff spot of psycho-analysis." What had
that got to do with this? The boy, her new lover,
would be antidote, cure, heal-all. Wasn't it better
simply to take another lover? At least, then, one
carried on the continuity. What would the new
pin-prick of analysis show in the depth of her unconscious? Why was Renne, Neil's sister, always so
intolerably logical, while Neil drifted, with the
breath of meadow-sweet, intolerably as illogical?
Certainly, sustained contact with the steel-brain of
Renne, her friend, had flung her finally into com-
mitting herself to marriage with Neil, the butterfly
brother, yet butterfly with platinum-lined intention

35

and again unpredictable sternness. Scotch, she supposed, anyhow Celt; the enigma.

This boy, David Leavenworth, was, thank God, Saxon, Empire-making, British. He was soft with that loam and oak and silly bull-dog-like stupidity. She was amazed at his English middle-class illiteracy that insisted on her "Americanisms," things they had for so long, in their world, taken utterly for granted. Well, bull-dog! It would help her to vilefy or re-habilitate the wily Highlands. Neil was out of the world, anyway.

Hadn't they always been out of the world? Wasn't that the reason that she could condone unfaithfulness, that flung Neil, by his own confession, "back into the old rhythm?" Perhaps she had been as intolerable to him, as he to her. Anyway, there was some super-blunder, or else he was sensitively cruel like a fine Damascus (was it?) blade. Did he, really, realise that the thing that had finally decided her, on this problematical "cure," was the fact of his taking this new-found Jerry, yes actually, back to their own terraine? Amalfi, God knows, is obvious, in all conscience, but why that little peak above an olive-island, that one tiny oasis in the panorama of the common-place, their own Sant' Angelo? Holy Angel, indeed! Was Neil angel or devil? Italianated—not quite! His post-card with "the geraniums still make

the whole cliff, card-board" was the very post-card
they had broadcasted by the dozen, because it was
so funny. Why, just that card? True, the Neapolitan
summer-visitors would have about cleaned out the
Signora Tommasa's revolving-frame, by this time.
To the right, was the cigar-stand and the box for
letters. Weren't there thousands of places, all of
Capri, for him to take his boy to? "Neil," she said,
then, "Neith." O, I am Natalia, this terrible Sia-
mese-twin that she and Neil had been. Yes, let Neil
grow a new obvious, geranium set of wings, in place
of the platinum and blue, she matched with. She
would grow wings, too.

This boy, David, had a hardy body. He said, he
was inexperienced. What anyhow, is experience?
Natalia pushed him away. He was not so young.
There must be delicacy in his approach to the thing
platinum-and-blue had loved. No, he mustn't wreck
her. His whole life might depend (this now, the
dynamic issue) on how she let him take her. She
might mould him into something sensitive, fine, tender (God knows, the women of England could do
with a few good lovers) or he might, in a few years,
harden into one of those smug, athletic, Empire-
building Englishmen. He was not so young. Or had
his experience been more than ordinary, inspired?
How did he know this? She said, "this never hap-

pened to me before." He said, "it never happened before to anyone, like this. This is the first time, it ever happened."

Well, that. How did he say that? Where did that come from? Neil, in his most effective moments, couldn't have bettered David Leavenworth's "this is the first time it ever happened." To him? No, obviously. Or was he only an instrument; was he, in his dark negation, a sort of conductor for some force? She must not let the metaphysical content, though, spoil this. No, David's was a clay body, or a David, at best, hewn by Angelo, from stone. Had Neil a body? Wasn't Neil arrogantly, trying to assert brutality, through sheer self-defence? What did it all matter? If she could "let go," as David was insisting, everything would come right. But would everything come right? O, just for a silly post-card, go on, go on Natalia, work it out, spin it out, let the intellectual factor that you so bewail in Renne, spoil all this. O, Natalia, think it out and spoil it, soil it, deface it, but don't do one and the other; think or let it go. She let go.

Spoil everything for the broken promise ("we won't write") and a flippant post-card. No, nor should Renne spoil it. She would tell Renne, of course. Without Renne, this, obviously, couldn't have been. The very repercussions that had flung her from Renne's over-clear way of thinking, now hurled her again, by a secondary series of fatal reactions, into the arms of a perfectly impossible person, a middle-class youth, their guest, spinning out his vacation and now perhaps flattering himself that, at any rate, he was "earning his keep." Well, it can't, anyway, last long. He will have to go back. One might as well take fully, if at all. She took fully.

Yet what had she taken, really? Another dimension, a place where Neil could never take her, a world of warm sand and silt on lake floors and the weed, across shallow pools. Neil was the platinum note of nature, lightning, frost on bracken, the pattern of molecules, moving in radiations, through glass, under a lens. Neil magnified and de-humanized and his sort of beauty sterilized all other beauty. Did it? Should it? David had said, "this is the first time, it ever happened" and it was as if a safety-curtain came down, bang in the middle of her being, dissociating Neil's Natalia from David's . . . Where is this taking her? Notes rise from under the floor, domed music. A dome spreads over and domes superimpose darkness upon darkness. Pray God, Neil's lightning doesn't strike through domes of music, domes of sand, darkness. Is she buried now, safe-dead? She is lying under sea-level, she says, "I am lying on a sea-floor." Her words are part of three columns of dark music, struck, muffled (a heart?) under her hand. She is rooted in silt and sand; even if she wanted to rise up, she dared not, for that destructive memory of heat-lightning across ice-floes. The "I love Neil" was lightning across ice-floes. Their love was too intensely cerebral. She had succeeded, almost, in snapping the ice-flower from the stalk, and when Neil could no longer endure her, she fell, drowning, to be caught. Such creatures lurk on the silt of the sea-floor.

"*Don't kiss me like that—again—*"

"*Why don't you call me David? You never say my name.*"

"*You haven't a name, you aren't now, David.*"

"*I am, I am. Nat. You do care?*"

"*No. I told you, quite frankly, in the beginning that I don't love you.*"

"*You do love me.*"

"*No. I told you in the beginning.*"

They repeat this, with slight variations. Canopy opens, closes, terrific force of that black. They are unborn, sentient only to the inner, black lining of the earth body. They have no names now, no identity. He will spoil everything if he insists on names, this fissure of personality. He will ruin the thing she is, the thing she lets herself be. Her hands creep along the torse that is Angelo Titan, not yet hewn out. She notes slight flabbiness of muscles. His arms are perfect and the arch of his back, is already personified, cast in bronze. The torse is not yet finished, there is flabbiness here, it must be beaten down, pounded in the clay. He says, "don't hurt me there, don't claw at me that way." She says, "I wasn't hurting you. I want to get you perfect."

Now, for a moment, everything is perfect. She is with him, under him; he is dead weight, but, again, her irresponsible body gets out. Weed-pennants sway above the weight of his head; it should be snapped off. It is a rock, lying on sea-floor.

"That stream outside, and all this, has worked some funny mystery. I don't know what."

"We must leave it alone, not plan anything, let it take us."

"Yes."

"If one plans, it doesn't work, always. We won't force anything. I want what you want."

Voices, coming from caves, sound hollow; small sound of echo of echo of voice sounds over the static quiet of the place, and the stream that eats along, under their very-sea, is one of those fabulous currents that run from antique mainlands, to thrill up into fountains, in the centre of hot island markets. The stream is such a stream, fresh water, against their salt. *I only want what you want.*

She has to come back, sometime. After all, I must get back to my room and last night that wretched Norridge would get up and prowl on the roof. Edna Norridge gets restless here; who wouldn't? If one could help this house-keeper, governess type of English women, but they flare out; internal combustion is all too spontaneous. Natalia does not now know what voice utters banal syllable, "it's the Norridge, I must get back between her prowls." But he does not hear her, her words are alien to him, "but I must go."

The body is solid enough, Angelo fountain-monster, half-carved. Her eyes are wide open to parallelogram of shadow and light, in bars, on his ceiling. There is the usual hoot of that car; motors, a tram and sometimes a distant train-whistle draw her from sea-depth. She counts something that is, again, his heart. She is standing by the window.

"*But you can't go.*"

"*Look. It's so beautiful.*"

She whispers, "beautiful, beautiful, beautiful," all to herself now. His shoulder will heave and rock hers, like avalanche from unknown crater. After all, she has been down in an unfamiliar cavern, and her world, her own terraine is just that—"beautiful, beautiful, beautiful." The air from the open window is more firm than she is; she could fall and be held there, by air; it is platinum edged with frost. Ground-mist follows the stream and blots out the stems of the paper-birches. This might be anywhere.

She wants suddenly, as David's shoulder touches hers, as her mind had predicted, to fall out, forward into platinum. Her own element has despised her, or was Neil really any element, as personifiable as frost? Wasn't he rather moist air with rainbows in it, catching colour from the near thing? Her own luminous lack of colour had sustained him, as Renne had at first sustained him, but a refracting mirror must have something other than clear silver to throw back. David was red of some fire under the world. Well . . . David!

She wants suddenly to make it somewhere, this surcharged darkness is all-earth. She wants to be established on the surface of this. She wants to talk in a banal way to a banal person. To-morrow will go on like yesterday and there will be no break in continuity, no ripple on the surface to show the Norridges of this world, where they have been. She wishes, for a moment, she could stabilise it, look forward to some simple, silly thing, an excursion to the Rialto or some hunt through Florentine byways, for a shop to mend her ear-rings. She wants to see herself, as silly as that, with ear-rings, not disembodied, with silver before her and inchoate rock at her back, at best to give her support . . . until she could find Neil ready to re-assure her. But she must turn, thank David Leavenworth, or say that she is sorry or say that she is glad, or kill him. She turns, though her hands try to stretch backwards, to that almost solid wall of pure air, while he bends her elbows to him. He nails her there with those muscular, strong feet. "Don't kiss me. If you kiss me, I can't go. There, I can sleep." He says, "stay here." She says, "I can't sleep. I told you, I didn't love you." He said, "you do now."

Why, this is David Leavenworth, their guest; it was Neil really asked him. Why, he might have been Neil's friend. Natalia knows, unhappily, that the old easy standards (wife-lover-mistress) have gone down. What, now, could hold any of them to life? There was Renne with no wings, or dragon-fly points, no sheltering wings nor breadth of colour, just needles to stab in you. "There is Renne." "But Renne," the inchoate thing said, "won't mind," and Natalia wondered what on earth she had said to this boy who was a young Empire-builder in embryo, and their guest. "No, Renne knows—this."

But Renne didn't know the least bit of this, Renne was all brain and such swift flash of needle-wing thought, that she seemed colourless. Was Renne a sort of mosquito, then, really? How could anyone

44

live, who didn't know this? But what did she, Natalia, know—only—surely it was not a failure! Why, she had almost got "out," she had never been so "out of the world" with Neil, but it was another world, this was the catch, she was "out" in.

"You're happy, you're not disappointed?" His feet close down on hers on the bare floor, he nails her there with his feet and she wants to get out; thank God, he is well-bred enough to act, to-morrow, as if nothing had ever happened. She wanted Renne to come in with her morning breakfast and she wanted —no, of course, Neil had said he wouldn't write and she had said, "so much better, don't write." It was all Neil's fault, sending that stupid post-card.

And Renne could say, vivisecting brilliantly with the shuttle of her brain, cutting back and forth through live woof, "you only love your mother in Neil," or just as logically, "you only love your father in Neil"; anyhow Renne said, "you're all out of proportion. You know Neil has that everlasting pre-occupation. If he loved his boys sufficiently and dynamically, he wouldn't—it wouldn't be Neil. He's a sort of mother to them." "You mean he—wants—?" "I've told you a thousand times, that would spoil everything. If you have his child then *you* are woman, *he* is man, that's smashed." Well yes. But wasn't it, she asked Renne, smashed anyway? Renne came back with her usual final volley, "he'd be all right with a spot of good analysis."

Leaving her, presumably, where she had been. It was obvious that all Natalia wanted, could possibly

cope with, was the living present. If Neil crept back
into her being, she would go mad. "Why would you
go mad?" Renne asked her. "Don't you see the
whole thing is abnormal? You never minded Neil's
friends before." No, but—but— wasn't it in the early
days of their marriage, then, before their marriage?
Don't people change with loving? Hadn't it really
been perfect in the beginning, their butterfly contact, the long walks and days in the burning sunlight, under that sky? Maybe, she herself, had been
too physically insistent. Then Renne said "guilt"
and "you really would do well to carry on with
David." O God! Renne!

Renne took it all on a purely psycho-surgical basis,
a cure for an illness, work it out of your system. Was
Renne right?

No. David was a root. Natalia needed that root.
She sank so far down, that even the transcendental
image faded. She could say, think consecutively,
Neil is not here. True, the very power of her negation, seemed in some way, to project him in some
other region of reality. Dark curtain, black glass,
shadow of alien planet, black-shadow across the
moon seemed to promise depth of new vision, once
lifted. It was as if the very moon-eclipse predicted
clearer visions. "*Nat, you do care.*" "*No. I told you
quite frankly in the beginning that I don't love you.*"

47

"*You do now.*" "*No. I told you in the beginning.*"

And this is quite true. This remains true. No. I told you quite frankly in the beginning. Perhaps now she can say, "I do care," for the black shadow had moved, anaesthetic, across a wounded surface. The black outline of the new lover stood between herself and the too rarified projection. Was Neil, himself, seeking some such escape, some such other-fulfil-ment, now on some moon-ridged cytisus ledge of their own Saint' Angelo? She could see, hear the new rhythm, the low sweet way of speaking, the sweet way of thinking that became at a moment obscene, corrupt, evil. Was Neil evil? Didn't he really want only to spare himself, the too rarified projection? Natalia could not stand the easy ribald talk between the brother and eclectic sister. But Renne was true to a new tradition; after all, their tradition and training had been different. The real pain, Renne predicted, had nothing to do with any conventional-ised love formula. It went back to some nursery-shock, some ill-tempered nurse or relative or even harassed and stricken parent. Natalia couldn't get back that far . . . yet . . . "David."

"Yes, darling. You are glad I came?" "So glad, David." "You're happier, to-night?" "Much hap-pier." "You, really, are very happy?" "O, really, very happy." For the moment, it is true, all that

Renne told her. The actual motivated act of love, was nothing, compared to the tenderness, the care he gave her. Was David substitute for some kindlier being, who, after the pain of some early suppressed sorrow, had taken her into wood and water, com‑forting? . . . But now it would be blasphemous to vivisect the miracle.

His weight was level, his weight was proportioned to hers. Her body was obliterated but his weight was proportioned, only the high arms sheltered a head, that somehow remained fixed, a head apart; a huge centaur clasped a head, dismembered in dry loam, from broken torse. He held her head; it had been discovered, he had kissed loam from the mar‑ble. His lips had enclosed her nostrils, so that she fainted into blackness. His mouth, closed over her mouth. He breathed into her, his breath had to be caught; strangling, she cried, "you must let me breathe." She forgot to breathe, shook shoulders, gasped, "make me come back, I must breathe."

He said, "well, breathe," and her gasp brought in silver of the stream outside (they were in her room) and the yellow plaques of the first fallen leaves. There was red‑bronze too, but her teeth savoured none of these things. There was fallen acorn and chestnut, broken to disclose nut and velvet lining and pods and red coral-berry, in the hedges. Her teeth tasted none of these things. There was loam and a stone head, scraped up by a hoof and a mouth coming back, coming back, "don't kiss me, let me breathe." "Well, breathe, then."

She swallowed the stream that whispered, sang, rhymed one couplet; the stream sang, whispered, sang. She drew that into her, so that she was drawn back and he held that water. She would so run be-tween the rock shelter of rock arms, so run on and on, run to meet bliss, be lost. But not now. She would wait; her marble, broken head blocked the run of stream-rhythm. "Rest, won't you." He would not let her go, embarrassment of letting her go, "it's all right, I love all that, don't worry, lie down now." He moved across her. He was giant-child, she must help him. He said, "but you—can't I—help you?" She said, "no." She must wait with a blue-lavender, refracted light now eating its way up across her right thigh. She would wait, apprehend that light. David would soon go.

"You're sure, you don't want—" "No, darling, this is a dream, let me keep this dream." The room was patterned with light from high-powered arc-lamps outside. The road turned here swiftly, toward a considerable lake-town. Here, they were alone on an isolated island. The hill made island of them, cut, here, by considerable town-road, there, by that stream.

He fumbled in his good-bye; across the pattern of blocked light, huge giant form fumbled; doorknob made the faintest echo. He took time over that. He stepped outside and closed the door imperceptibly, but slowly so that she waited one more, tense moment. He was gone now. She waited for the same half-echo of a shut latch from his room.

Her deity was impartial; as the radium gathered electric current under her left knee, she knew her high-powered deity was waiting. He would sting her knee and she would hold muscles tense, herself only a sexless wire that was one wire for the fulfil-ment. She was sexless, being one chord, drawn out, waiting the high-powered rush of the electric fer-vour. It crept up the left side, she held it, timed it, let it gather momentum, let it gather force; it escaped her above the hip-bone, spread, slightly weakened, up the backbone; at the nape, it broke, distilled ra-dium into the head but did not burst out of the hair. She wanted the electric power to run on through her, then out, unimpeded by her mind.

She would be a spirit, Saint' Angelo, Saint Angel, and Neil would be a spirit. In heaven, there is assur-edly, no marriage nor giving in marriage. If she were a Christ, she would use, distribute this power; she would think only holy thought; she would be purified like a clod of earth, drawn up into the radiant texture of some fragrant lily. Weren't they all, in their way, experimentalists in this very-vibrant power, this holy radium? Maybe they were wrong, it was so easy to sink back into that cycle of terror and guilt.

She was happy to find her face, salt-wet with tears. Mind yet checked the flow of white electricity. But she was nearer than she had ever been to the source of this power. Evil? Sin was the damning of this force until it ate back into the fibre of existence, turned foul, in spite and suppression of maniacal repudiation. Yet how judge? She hated the spend-thrift of beauty, as much as the miser. Each must find his own high-road to deity. To-night, she was not far off.

Renne would say, father-fixation and religious mania.

NIGHT III

        ... the Greek is radium. The Egyptian
is the gold beetle, the Greek the white, escaped
butterfly ... She saw no force for it but death, and
as the aura of radiant life sped through her, she saw
that she was not so much healed as shocked back,
re-vivified, for fresh suffering. Would she die sometime in some such shock-aura of pure light? And if
so, would she be flung into a mediaeval hell, filled
with the most hideous of refuse, come to life, the
horrors of the unconscious? Was her fervour, after
all, an illicit escape, an inhuman intolerance of the
casual, tiresome things of this life? Should she have
Neil's children?

Has she broken into the sheep-fold and if so, what
of it? What wrong had she done? Maybe Renne was
right, though, if Nat found out *why* she did these
things, perhaps she need not suffer. But her aptitudes

are many and she is glad to be alone in her own bed.

She has found again, that the dream is more important. The shawl has tassels over her silk sleeping-coat. The coat is soft against her shoulder, her sleeves and the silk fringe of the shawl are dull rose. The shell in her hand is pearl. Out of the hollow of the shell (held, reflecting the blurred edge of the upper inset line of concealed wall-lights) her world begins. It will begin. Her shell will begin. When the shell is focussed at the required angle, it will begin. She waits; the stream makes background; across it, cut the sophisticated sounds of motor cars, hooting as they round that corner to the not inconsiderable lake-town, some miles along the lake edge, further. Her mind collects impression, the modern lighting of her symmetrical box of a room, the wind in the line of paper-birches that follow that stream, doors up and down the corridor and finally the last slam as Miss Norridge goes to bed. Neil is in Italy. Renne has flung military brushes and pyjamas in a suit-case and followed Una, her exotic friend, to Paris. David has gone to fit them properly in their compartment on the Orient Express, and now they'll have Una's companion-secretary, la Barton, as they call her, on their hands. I may fall asleep before David gets back.

54

Nat waits while the rumble of the tram cuts over the stream sound; that train is never on time. She will collect her mind, concentrate on outer circumstances. The stream is miracle, the tram and the personal hoot of somebody's Citroën are miracle. They are imposing Piccadilly, Kurfürstendamm, Fifth Avenue on the magic of the Clairmount, on the autumn moon that rises, too stupidly dramatic, the stream that holds it down, insinuated into all their picture. Out of the shell . . . out of the shell.

The flat, Pacific abalone shell, gives back patterns. This pattern is assembled in her mind, it glows out, then her heart stops and her breathing. There is a crude shaped statue, seated on a ledge of stone. The columns are not Greek, they are not Egyptian. Nat's breath holds, her sharp sense goes out, she feels the shell is living. As her eyes focus, her head melts, the hard silver of convoluted brain is molten. In its place is a cloud substance, sustaining it; vision. Her vision predicts Greek, out of Aztec. She finds the columns are carved with no known hieroglyph. There is an intensified, tall, slight statue. This woman must turn.

There is a door and a purple hill-slope, cut into layers, purple, green. There is a hill-slope that intensifies itself and the door of this temple is set on a ledge of water. It is some inner, undiscovered Aztec dwelling; the small statue is upright, delicate, un-classified. Nat will hold this. It will, she knows, turn under her vision, a butterfly wing under micro-scope, turn and fling out Protean syllable. It will turn to Greece, to Egypt. There is a hatted figure, seated, with long knees, at the rise of the first cataract. The rocks might be Arizona or mid-north America. The stream is the Nile; this changes, shifts, light on a blue wing.

She is back in Greece, an island; the woman, will not turn round. Her heart leaps out towards the woman who will not turn round and the curve of her spine tells that story, tells how Natalia herself had lain last night, her emotion spreading electric aura, so that she lay in the white sheet-lightning of her aura. An aura must be fastened like butterfly, like angel wings to a naked, scraped spine.

Flesh must be scraped off, we must eat what will make us live. The woman became pre-Ionic, gross, with large breasts, she looked out, over another stretch of water. The hooting of a motor-car made Nat wonder, "has David got back?"

David would come back, would sit there; she switched off the light, forgetting David.

He walked into her, out of the shell, stepping into half-light, like a centaur or a negro. She was wide awake at his entrance, her eyes saw simply her room, the usual squares of familiar, bright light in the black, inner surface of her modern little box-room. The wide doors, opening on the terrace, are as wide as the wall opposite and curtains drawn in heavy fold, make any entry an entrance. David has entered, wide shoulders bent, like a centaur or a negro.

"*You are out of this shell.*"

"*Yes,*"

"*You are out of this shell.*"

She still holds the abalone shell, as when she fell asleep, half covered, tangled in the shawl fringe. He says, "they got off all right," but Nat has forgotten Una and Renne. He says, "I wish I could sleep with you all night, just stay, quietly, like this." His shoulders are not real shoulders, they are part of miracle, he is not a man, never could be David. They are rock to her grasp, as hard and firm as the edge of Nile, the rock, below the cataract, the rock of the mid-American canyon and the ledge of the Aztec temple. She wants to tell him of this, say, "you did so much for me, have done, you make me get into all sorts of lights, vibrations, you know." He may not understand but he understands a rock, a butterfly, and he leans over her. His mouth, too, is out of that shell, his kiss is mid-earth volcano, heat of glowing

57

red-hot coal, out of earth-heart. Such red coal keeps alight, on an Aztec altar. He will probably not understand her; he does not, he says, "I want to sleep quietly with you," he does not realise that she is not clutching, with any woman greed, at those shoulders, that his strength is ledge of stone, altar; she says, "yes—go," he says, "you are holding me," but she says, "you can easily get away, you can always break away from my arms." He does not like to seem to break away, so she lets go. He does not understand, though he apprehends, that he is out of her shell. She says, "I was making such pictures, it all came clear. I hardly understand, myself, but you understand. Do you understand?"

He turns, he leaves her, he is standing in the doorway. He says, "Renne said, would I tell you to look after Felice Barton. She'll be lonely without Una, and upset. If la Barton takes it into her head to act up, it's all up with Una and Renne." Nat heard the words that needn't have been spoken, of course they would waylay the Barton, inflict themselves on her; invidious and incorrigible, they would spread out Renne like a patterned Persian carpet, she is this, she is that, Renne will be just the person at the moment for poor, harassed Una.

"Renne thinks we better both take on la Barton." "Of course." Una is there, too, out of the shell, there is some kind of Una-unicorn or that Spenserian lion, some sort of Tarot symbol that has got lost. Una was one of the Arcana, as they call them, of the Tarot, detached from the pack. She would shuffle all their values. ''Of course—Una—''

It was so much a matter of course, that people stood around, like tents, now. She must crawl back into her covering, her shell, see herself as inhabiting a shell, Natalia, crawl out, become Neith from some cataract rock-edge, go further, become incohate lining of the very earth, spring up again at a command, an inhibition, some freak of chance that would drag out a maid to prowl down the corridor or that would prompt Edna Norridge, at midnight, to fasten or unfasten an embarrassing window. These things rippled the surface, were so much drift-weed and spind-drift.

But there were moments when she must combine several moods, re-value herself and in so doing, cast a more humane, mature eye over the rest of the assembly. Renne, for instance, was solidly incarnate in her husk; she wallowed in her sturdy personality like an eskimo, in a mud-lined ice hut. Outside,

Renne was ice; inside, turmoil of desire and suppression; she wallowed in her suppression like an eskimo in the lining of smoke and tallow. Una seemed to live in some nomad shelter of wicker and boughs. She wandered, she carried her belongings and her self with her. She could hardly be detached from the dryad quality of the self she lived in.

Felice Barton was like an overblown queen of hearts or (Tarot) queen of cups. Natalia had made headway with la Barton over an unearthed heap of fortune-cards. Felice was one of those blighted queens of hearts or cups. She was all bounty and twisted mother-compound. They were all her daughters, but there was no bitterness in her love of women. She had her own children, anyway.

Now Felice had gone home.

It was odd that David should sit, staring at her, over her typewriter. She lifted the machine from the low, crowded table, pushed books aside, reached for his hands. His hands lay on hers, heavy, dominant, "you love Mrs. Barton?" She was startled. "But why, David?" Was it possible that he was jealous? "I feel it. She tapped something in you, she punctured something in you." He understood, in his ridiculous way, everything; things she herself couldn't cope with. "No, she didn't. I mean, it was talking about those cards." They sit, face to face, across a desk, a counting-house table. The type-writer, the books, make it an office table. "Did Mrs. Barton catch the le Lac bus?" "She decided to walk back."

The face is nearer, nearer. The eyes are wide, black, they are wide, startling eyes in the solid contour of the heavily-modelled face. The face is earth, the eyes, black up-starting flowers, laden poppies. The eyes deepen, with the soft powder of the drug. "You love women. I'm always afraid that you will love some woman. Una liked you really. Do you love Felice Barton?" Eyes, eyes, eyes, eyes spring over and beyond them; eyes on apocalyptic wings are drug that will beat out her life. Why does he suggest these things? She struggles through the web of eyes that beat about her, apocalyptic wings, and eyes, says flippantly, "of course, I love her, naturally, why not?" and watches him quivering from her. She is spider, stabbing butterfly-wing full of black eyes. She sees herself, sees himself, humanises. She is human, flippant, "you are so easy to tease, David. Of course, I love Felice Barton, don't you? Felice is emotionally blousy, like an overblown cabbage-rose, any bee or butterfly could hum there. Who wouldn't love Felice? Do you?" He says, "of course," hard, conventional, he is young, incarnate

Englishman, she is startled, starts up, "you *love* Felice?" They are staring; they laugh. She opens Natalia-eyes, David is sitting near her, the English face now Titian; fur would become his collar. The chin is soft, rounded, now she sees the eyes do not change, are two, simply, poppies out of bed-rock.

"You don't want me, then?" "I didn't say I didn't want you." "Could I come back, just to say good-night, just for five minutes?" "You mean—" "Yes, I won't be tiresome." She slips from a chair, undoes a scarf. He catches at the silk. She binds the stuff over his eyes. The face is common-place, the mouth over-sensual, she has hidden the eyes. "Well—come back for five minutes, then."

Now she will tell him; he has enclosed her in his arms; she will tell him. "I didn't draw away, David. I wanted to tell you." He says, "then, I didn't do you good? I wasn't a good doctor?" She says, "yes, yes. Don't you see. I couldn't give myself, not give myself so early like that, all at once. After you left—after you left—"

"After I left?" "I was excited. I waited for a long time. Then I excited myself more." His arms tightened. "I didn't," she said, "take anything away from you, for I couldn't have given you that." She said, "it was almost sexless. It was almost automatic contraction. It was white and lavender. It was radium. I wanted to get out of my body." He said, "you did get out of your body."

He says, "I want either to have you all, or sleep here, one or the other." "You best go." He said, "I want to stay." He sat on the edge of her bed, his shoulders were there, heavy as usual, his hand seeking her hand. He pressed it to his lips, like any continental lover. He would go, "in at the door, out at the window," like any lover of low comedy. *David.*

His mouth lay over hers, as she stopped breathing. Her breath was taken into his body, then she stopped breathing. Blue fire crept, like Michaelmas mist, up out of the darkness, there was the usual solid columns of white pillars, seen far distant in a blue mist. The mist solidified, it would solidify into lapis, into Mediterranean mid-night blue. She would go out, out into the mid-night blue (if she stopped breathing) and walk into the familiar corridor. He withdrew his mouth, shook her, so she must breathe. "Do you know when I stop breathing?" He answered, "always."

She drew life back in the drowning gasps that she had learned from him. She had found out in those few contacts, what now to do. "I know two things, these make love for me." He said, "you were really frightened then, when I loved you so terribly. Did I hurt you?" She said, "you did hurt me, the terror was part of it, the unfulfilment and the terror, the nearness, the unfamiliarity and the recognition of a familiar terror." He said, "then you didn't really want it?" She said, "the terror and unfulfilment drove me right out. I was frightened, but I got out." She waited to hear him say, "this will be bad for your heart," or "this will be dangerous," but he didn't say it. "How do you understand all these things?" . . . the drug poppy in his eyes was contradiction of his solid incarnation.

He was solid and he would hold her. She could let go, because he was solid and knew the technicality of heart-beat and the vibrations of the life-rhythm. She could go out, get out. His lips would open her mouth, his eyes would drop their poison, she would drink the poison of the earth-flower that drew power from the earth-heart. She would lie in his arms, die, be so blotted into darkness. His lips would open her mouth, breathing the darkness that was sleep, that was oblivion; his rooted-stalk would push down. Those other lips would be penetrated by the slow poison of that beating earth-flower, down and down, into her drugged body. He would break anew a wound, work into a cauterized wound, to renew and re-create. He would work into her, fertilize, invoke that flower.

She had worshipped that dark bloom, he had brought fervour to it. "I went almost too far, I almost got out of my body." He said, "you did get out of your body."

NIGHT V

Now she knew she was in many pieces and that she was not there. Una, for a whim, had shortened the short Paris week-end; she and Renne were back already, and Una was already talking of going on. Una would dash erratically across the Continent. Prague? Vienna? Una was perverse, lost, unhappy. The amber eyes stared out and light, behind them, was light in a coptic crypt. She was dead really, in her way. Una was dead. Una would die of faithfulness. Women were mad to go on that way, about women.

Una stared, keeping alight something that smouldered on a coptic altar. Love was all right. Why didn't she make it up, get along with Renne? Faithfulness would turn arid or wouldn't it? Was Una's the last test of love endurance, was her crown final? Crown upon crown—Una was love martyr.

"But have your cocktail, Una." But she wouldn't. She stared out and out. No wonder Felice worried. Renne must take her in hand—Vienna.

Una lit tapers in a coptic crypt, she sat there in Neil's room and brought Neil back. Why burn tapers to the dead? Neil was safe. Neil had gone off. It was Neil who was unfaithful. Una? Certainly Una never had been. O, damn Una. Natalia swept out with collected cocktail glasses on a tray, and stumbled with them in the lower hall. It was the Norridge's fault really, she shouldn't have had that tooth-ache. Nat was in shattered pieces. She stood looking down at David in his dark silk pyjamas. "Damn Una."

"Why Una, at this moment?" "She broke my nerve. I broke those damn sea-green glasses that Neil loves so." "Well, he can get some others." David didn't see the significance of it, that she was wantonly destroying herself or destroying Neil, that she had stumbled on purpose somehow, that she hated the meddling of the unconscious impulse. Neil was being swept up, bits of him under the carpet, and here and there a green fragment to stare up like a jewel or to cut your feet coming in, from the garden or from the lake side. She had, self-consciously, flung the thing down; of course, she hadn't stumbled. She had shattered that love.

"Won't you get in, Nat?" "No, I came in to say good-night. I don't want to spoil things. Anyhow, you're worried." He was worried about letters, something to do with his work in London, something he didn't tell her about and that she didn't want to speak of. "I wish I knew how Neil is." She stood, looking down at him in that sleeping jacket, almonds flung across boulders. He was sweet and strong, young, old, mother, child, father, friend. What wasn't David? She would be perverse, stare down, torture herself, tease him, "it's those hateful glasses."

The hand was on her knee. She wanted to fall, be alabaster, let herself be shattered. Such light had burnt for Neil, as burns in alabaster. She had burnt white flame for Neil, and Una, with her damned homosexuality, had kept that other light burning in a secret crypt. Una had been mad and faithful for years to a girl that didn't matter. Was this homo-sexuality at fault, then? Had Nat really loved the tall girl in Neil? Was she angry when that went? Men must grow up, he had been so incredibly bal-anced, that a breath the wrong way, and he was quite gone. I can't be faithful to a peaked middle-ageing old maid. O God—Neil!

The arms were around her knee, David was going to pick her up, set her down, somewhere else. The wind was howling about the porch of a temple, but the temple was shattered (those cocktail glasses) and she was left standing, incredibly ridiculous, a torn bit of drapery flapping where curtains had been. She was exposed to wind, to rain, to hail now. "You're shivering."

"It's those glasses."

She held on to the iron bed-rail, like someone blown sideways in a gale. She talked across the howling of that wind, "Renne has been beautiful; we must do everything we can for her and Una." She was out of all this really, had failed both ways, might have gone on, completed a relationship with Renne, might even have been of some use to Una— men! She looked down on the thing that would save or wreck her. She looked down at the heavy body, saw the face; don't look at the eyes.

She would wait for him to change expression, she would take her clue from it. His eyes were black, that British blue drowned out. There wasn't any thing to distinguish him from any ardent athlete. There was a classic stupidity about the wide brow and the hair, ridiculously fine and tending to stand upright, with a silly rather terrier-curl. His hair was like dried grass and the hair of a small terrier. It was too short, ever to be anything but tidy, except for these whisps. She rounded his head with her hand, felt grass along a boulder. "Well—" "Well—" "Aren't you going to say good-night?"

"Aren't you going to say good-night," meant, aren't you going to be a decent chap (as he would say) rouse out of that torpor, switch off the light? She knew what he meant, shook out of that mood, walked over an unsteady floor. She was paralyzed, now the light was off, wondered how she would get out of her slippers, said, "I've got on slippers." He was holding back the covers, the bed-clothes were banked like the dim lining of a tomb. Was bed, tomb; womb? Would she walk into life now, or would life now reject her? Una.

"I won't offer you violence." He was making a joke in the conventionalised manner, soon he would say, "be a decent chap, come on." She would be a decent chap, shake out of a sterile negativism— would she? Would she lose everything again—or gain? He had her hand, bent it, palm upward. He had turned her palm up, was kissing the back of her hand. His mouth was bull-sensuous. She crawled in. He said, "if you'd only sleep, not worry." His palm was solid, and his fingers. The fingers were mechanically jointed and firm as iron. That iron hand was lined with magnetism, like a glove. "I won't sleep." He said, "if only you would; why can't you just sleep?'' He thought she was sleepy, would sleep, as she sank down.

She was in so many pieces. The hand held her; she was in many, many pieces. The fingers held her, did not move, went taut, as her hand went limp and she herself allowed all the rest of herself to drift out, to become amorphous, while he held her. Had he saved her from this last, most desperate drowning or was there some other form of regeneration to be learned? Chemical change seemed to take place, as his mouth held hers. She seemed to breathe a new substance into her lungs like those ridiculous hydrangea roots that turn blue in—she couldn't remember what people poured over the earth, so that white hydrangeas were blue. Something was poured into her, volatile, potent as ether, that was turning the very marrow of her bones into another substance. He was melting her bones.

Personality was the thing that didn't matter. The first time she had said that, she had thought, ''David will break between *us* and make *him-me*, a fissure or a chasm.'' There was no chasm in this. It wasn't anything to do with any of them. Her mind went out, out. She realised one part unmolten—that hand. The hand was hand out of ashes, Pompeii. The hand was something apart, had a life of its own, a brain. His hand was thinking, ''Natalia is sleeping.'' She

wasn't asleep, just melted down into this other element. The hand moved, she felt her own arm emerge,
he dragged her out from drowning. She felt herself
go cold, static; electrocuted, dead corpse. She felt
death creep in. She was thinking of those glasses.

She could feel herself in many parts again, dyna-
mited to bits. Those glasses were too damn symboli-
cal. They had recalled, she remembered, the colour
of the flat wave. There were orange blossoms and
the reflected cypresses. That island was like a toy on
wheels, symmetrical, with peak and point and low
roof. There had been winter-oleanders in tubs. Neil!

Neil and Una (though they didn't personally
affiliate) stood for cypresses, the dead mermaid green
of the little Syren island, off Amalfi. Honeymoon.
What rot! Neil got so furious over nothing these
days. Renne was the only one who was impervious.
One's sister would be. Nat was more like Neil, really.
People thought Natalia was his sister. They were
too near, related really. David must save her from
this introversion. "David." "Darling." She would
come back, force herself out of this brittle Neil-
mood, talk about anything that happened. "I think
old Felice is like a plot of peonies, don't you?"
"You've been thinking about Felice?" "Felice."

She said "Felice" and began to laugh foolishly. "It
must be that hands do it, I mean dropping cocktail

73

glasses." He let her go on. "Perhaps when one was small, one got slapped?" It seemed from the beginning of time, one had been told not to touch things —*touch things*. Hands. His hands were reaching. Hands were reaching, superimposed on his hands. They re-valuated her torse. Here, they seemed to say, is authentic fragment. Hands.

There was a black sort of sweat that broke out. David knew all about it, he was so stolid but he knew that. He turned and his shoulders were windscreen, she lay under boulders. Over his left shoulder, wind howled and she dragged feet in, out of the cold. His feet found and pinned hers, rape out of stone-age. He was stone, out of stone-age.

NIGHT VI

Tired, tired, tired, tired, tired. She is so tired. She is neither incarnate nor re-incarnate, she is so glad la Barton and Una are due to leave to-morrow. "No," she had said, "I don't want to take the trip, please, David, keep Renne company. Go on with them." She had had enough of staged, dramatic good-byes, la Barton, sincere and hysterical, and Una, under the lamps at the drive, on the way back to their hotel, flinging a monocle into an eye and pressing an invitation. Una was suddenly pseudo-mondaine, for the first time.

She was glad they'd gone; already, as far as she was concerned; would actually leave le Lac to-morrow. She couldn't bear, any more, the self-conscious, yet so poignant elfishness of Una. Una would wreck any pre-conceived estimate of Una, chestnut-red-lion hair, the wide eyes opening to show darker brown like chestnut burrs, revealing dark kernel of the

75

fruit. Una's eyes stared wide, from the famous spikey lashes. All the things publicity allowed Una were tripled when one saw her. She was as simple (they were right there) as a child. Whether she had or had not slept once with a semi-detached wealthy Jew who was her husband, was nobody's and everybody's business. She was not even demi-vierge, was tiresomely Peter Pan. She stared with wide eyes until Natalia had said, "I know the sort of scenario you want, I know just the sort of screen thing." Natalia had to play up to the insistent and frightening demands of Una, all the time play up, not for the very obvious "advantage" of it, to herself possibly and certainly to Neil, but because there Una sat (with five wardrobe trunks and twenty hats, Mrs. Barton told them) in a woollen pull-over and flat shoes, demanding out of dark eyes, amber and honey and shadow on water—what? O God, Natalia did not want that, did not want this insistency of the half-wood, the shadow and the fragility of aspens. Una! O yes, she had said to Una, "I know what you want."

Then, against herself and her better judgment, she had outlined a simple phantasy of trees, where the trees would be superimposed on a face that was not man nor woman nor child. It was Una. And Una lapped it up, sat enchanted, as easy to charm her as any reptile, out of a hole in the wall, or battered fledgling. But Una was Renne's affair. Why did Renne's girl-lovers turn, as inevitably to her, as Neil's boys? Well, she had done her best and, at the end, brought down the wrath of a justly inflamed Renne. "But Renne, I don't want the infant. She's lost. She's lonely. She's horribly battered and spoiled. But she's authentic." Thank God, under la Barton's wing, Una would by this time, to-morrow, be well off.

David, thank God, had let Natalia go, in Renne's room, with a casual good-night. She had left him sitting on Renne's bed, holding forth about Felice, Una and le Lac in general, letting Renne feel that she, Renne, was all important and Renne was that. Renne was sitting against a coffee-coloured curtain, in fresh striped-rose pyjamas. She was sipping a weak lemon and brandy punch. David was curled up, in his ridiculous rug of a dressing gown at the foot.

O God, sleep, just to sleep . . .

Out of her head, there was still such a wild and evil medley. There was clatter and the ice-insistence of Neil. Nat wished she didn't dream, hadn't dreamed, that night that he had come jibbering, like one of the madmen out of the Duchess of Malfi, and

had jibbered till she had screamed in the night . . .
"*Neil*." Of course, it was all a muddle. It wasn't
anyone's affair, certainly not Neil's, that she should
want to break the continuity of that ice-terror and
just get warm. David was so simple. He was an
ordinary dull, well-bred, middle-class Englishman;
then his mouth covered hers . . . "Nat," he would
say and it would be Neit or Neith out of a Luxor
temple.

Nat was admittedly her name, Natalia for the
more purely civic and decorous occasion. "Nat," he
would say, Neith or Neit out of Luxor . . ."Nat,"
he did say, "O David, I thought I *had* said good-
night. I didn't hear you coming." "Sleeping?" "No,
half. I mean, not really." He flung himself down, in
that heavy dressing gown, "just one kiss," and she
knew that that one kiss would let slide some magic
panel, in the closed room of her heart. His kiss was
broken seal of one of the apocalyptic seven seals of a
book, some old, old manuscript, still rolled carefully,
no doubt, but in strips, buried under sand. When
David kissed her like that, her breath stopped and,
in a moment, the thread of the present was broken,
she was back in the past. His lips closed over her
half-open lips and she stopped breathing. "Where
did you learn to do that?" He said, "I never learnt it.
It happened." It happened now as she waited, even

in the kiss, for him to go. "I'm really so tired." "And I." "Listen. I must ask you to go. If you stay it will only upset us. It's so late. I get so tired, talking to Una." He echoed her "thank God, they're off tomorrow." "Yes not Una only, la Barton has some uncanny understanding. She lent me those German Tarots. We had such fun, we spread out all the cards and that diluted sort of Burne Jones English set I have." She saw the faces of the cards living, like Alice and her court suits. "David."

She would get out, under that kiss. It was possible that it would kill her. It was one of the Major Arcana of the Tarot. It might be 13, her favourite almost, Death and the other more intense meaning that the 13 gave it. She believed that David's kiss was death because there was only blackness as she dropped under it and it spread (when she stopped breathing) a black canopy over her head. The kiss was, in that sense, authentic. They were out of European, modern computation, white thoughts. Their thoughts were Egyptian, Indian, Hindoo, American Indian. They met in the Greater Arcana, there was no separating of body and spirit. How much could he know? Could he follow her right out? She must not let this come . . .

Simply incarnate, simply herself, in her green dressing gown, she was lying beside David. Simply herself with one day to the good, she was a fine outdoor person who had collected three dogs and met one of their owners on the way home. She had run the length of the lower road below the Clair-mount, run across levels, their valley, and stopped to breathe in the stream, scent of chestnut burrs, scent of different colour of leaves that lay, some copper gold, some mouse-brown and that again replaced their own virginal crispness by another savour, as she kicked through the top layer, and then brought to light the sodden leaves beneath them. Running toward the lower levels of the Clairmount, there had been that grey-hound, belonging to the people at Bas-Coin. It had a double set of tiny pointed wings to its hare-like heels, and ran on ahead to run back, so she had knelt down to see its collar and its nose had jerked her chin up, till she realised it had a jealous companion, another dog from somewhere, who curried favour, over and across the grey-hound. The second was no good for anybody's wolf-hound; such a hound, she had been taught to believe, bit strangers, led blind men across crowded pavements, a very well-bred guardsman among hounds. This one was friendly. It seemed to think it owned her, till the arrival of the ridiculous mongrel dachshund.

All that running among leaves . . . David.

"I've got you back." How strange of him to say that, when she was so far afield, when the small room did not hold her and she was limp there, for just this second, because she had promised to come in, to say good-night, after his special gladness to come back, after the long motor-run with Renne to put Una and Felice Barton properly, on their train. He had flung her a bundle of chrysanthemums, like tawny small lions. She had thanked him but come back to thank him again. How odd he was. He said she had come back, when she was so far afield with tiny hare-feet and wings, fastened to a grey-hound's neat heels. "Have I been away, then?" He said, "yes, the Barton did something to you." "I feel more *away*, as you put it, now than I have been for some time." He said, "I had your rather lovely body, but it was very empty." How did he know this? How did he know that Mrs. Barton had tapped something? "What do you mean about the Barton? You mean, we were so en rapport?" No, he didn't mean that, he said, "she took something from you." "It's so pleasant to have things—taken."

He said, "yes, but she punctured something, it wasn't your fault."

Yes, the Barton had done that, but how did he know? Nat let herself go limp, surprised at his intuition. Neil, of course, ought to know things like that, Nat had worked out the Barton's "numbers" from an old chart that Neil had inherited from some crazy second-sighted relative. The numbers worked and when she told the Barton this, this, be careful of that, the Barton was astonished. "It was just the usual clap-trap," she explained to David, "a little about numbers and modified sort of Tarot." He said, "you're terribly queer with these things." She admitted this, "I was tired; she would insist so; I just half-blurred myself out and things came." Nat didn't do this, ordinarily, for people; she was taken with the Barton, part Irish and married, before the war, to a German. The Barton had been through that. It was easy to predict, astonish anyone of that sort; it was near enough to her self. "Yes. She tapped something."

Don't go back, David, into what she so tapped.

That was so long past. There is this, the breathing and the shoulder that takes two hands to cling to . . . "It's more beautiful than I can tell you, that you trust me." She is so cool, so cold, so removed and running on wings into the lower sunlit hollows of the Clairmount, that she is not even conscious of his kisses; this kiss returns the night to her, this returns kingdoms. "I'm old," he says, "old; you're old, old, old," he says. He understands how the Barton and the playing cards tapped something, and he feels that she is nearer to-night, with the run of the lower Clairmount changing her veins to silver, then she was, those nights ago, seeming close, after talking to the Barton. She says, "to-morrow, or the next day." He says, "you'll come?"

He came too quickly but that was not his fault. He was, as he told her, shuddering against her shoulder, too terribly excited. She let go, let drown into blackness, she couldn't say it was all right, she was so frightened simply. He said, "it will be so bad for you. Just beginning—inhibition." She said, "it isn't that, it's only the pathological terror—did you—hurt me?" He said, "no, no. Please. It's all right." Then she sank back into terror.

It was a pity, he had come so suddenly. He had been exquisitely near her, poised; their contact, a dream. She dragged herself out, "listen. Sometimes the most beautiful dream is broken that way. Sometimes, on waking, there is a fragment of a fragment of a memory, the slope of a hill seen through crystal, the slope of a hill covered with violets or the slope of a hill, white with whitethorn or elderberry or one or two ghost-trees, stark smoke and ghost and spirit against a black edge of a wood." She knew that broken sort of astral-dream, where one woke and the poignant moment comes when one knows that all one's childhood has really been a perfect thing, because under and through it, though one did not understand and only vaguely sensed it, there was a path running to the sea and the sea-sand lay level, through some familiar wooded pasture. Suddenly, such a memory wakens one and one is sure that the whole of one's broken childhood and adolescence was—something. Over the mere husk, the jagged "self" that learnt incongruous letters and obsolete lists of numbers, there was another self that ran, that had run, day in, day out, along a sand-path, that ran on and on and on, through deep wood to rocks. The sea was always waiting.

"Listen. Don't feel badly. Sometimes the most beautiful thing is remembered, because it's broken." She did not feel resentful; this butterfly moment that she had held, had endured, perhaps, six heart-beats; in those slow heart-beats, she had known every-thing; just for that time, had realised perfection; they were so delicately poised and he seemed so sure. Of course, that tender almost imperceptible vibra-tion that had quivered while they held the moment static, was too much, the vibration was out of time,

beautiful. She held her courage, held on to something static. She said, "one must learn. You didn't
realise—we have been only these few times together." He was desolate, as a clumsy child, who
has broken fabulous crystal. She repeated, "the
most beautiful dream is remembered sometimes, because of the moment of its breaking."

She must not be afraid now. He must not realise
that she was frightened. She ran light hands across
the torse, those hands, he said, were hurting. She
said, "they can't hurt, I'm touching you so lightly."
He said, "if you had done this in the beginning—
before—I should never have dared love you." She
questioned, letting the hands go limp, a little won-
dering. "Your fingers are full," he said, "of the most
terrific electricity. I'm frightened." She could not
explain that it was a thing between them, the wire
he was, the wire she was, the positive and negative,
or something of that sort, nor discuss it in electrons.
She wanted him to know she forgave the breaking
of the crystal.

Then when he went, she remembered that the
dream is more important. When he went, she discovered that it was the dream that broke the fabulous crystal, that broke crystal to set more beautiful

ray about her. She saw the globe about her forehead and knew that in it, she saw everything. The dream waited. She apostrophised the dream, said, "I see that you broke that in order to give me greater," she saw David far off, saw Neil far off. David or Neil, they were only bridges, they led her to her dream, they were the rainbow arch, they were their own particular colour, or their own timbre or electron, but they were the bridge, were not the dream; she loved the dream. She spoke to the dream and her own vibrant deity was waiting.

The god was there. She knew his shape, his colour. He changed; Egyptian, Aztec, Navaho. If he were Red Indian, she knew the run of wood and the path that led on through forests. If he were Aztec, she was perfectly aware of the twisted carvings of the winged snake, of the very-particular sort of bent broken angle of a hybiscus-shaped sort of pattern, like acanthus. She knew this, this, this. If he were Egyptian, she would succumb to him in pleated transparent drapery, her body lithe as that snake, her mind luminous and bent only on its self expression. She must express herself in luminous electrons, say, "I knew it was you who touched the rod to blossom, broke off a small branch." She would know the gift and its withdrawal, it was he who had sent her David. For one moment, he had incarnated himself in David, drawn off. He was jealous. He was exact. He was exacting. He would fling lover upon lover to her, provided, she held conclusive—*the dream is greater than reality!*

Now she felt cold to David and she didn't want him. She escaped from that usual good-night, felt the warm beauty of the body, a body now and David. She had said, in the beginning, "I don't love you, and you aren't David." She knew, now, that the moment, last night, had been too perfect and he had been almost David.

But she didn't, now, want David. He would hold her, press kisses upon her, know all the time that she had drawn off. She could explain it, as she had that other time, say, "you see you excite me and, after you left, I excited myself more." But she didn't want to explain it. She must get away, must lie alone, must let lines and patterns and the two inter-locked triangles of light and shadow, like the draw-ing-book illustration of light and shadow, draw her out. She wanted to watch triangles of light and shadow, on her ceiling. She wanted to lie, parallel with a ceiling and she wanted to be a parallel, running to infinity and never touching that twin other-line. She wanted David there. But she must be free.

It was not his fault that he had come too quickly last night and now, wanting to make up, she was frightened. "No," she said, "you see"—and drew away, letting imagination reach over, let him think she had talked too long with Renne; she said, "you see, Renne with her panic about the crisis and all that, has upset me." She didn't care a damn about the crisis. All she wanted to know was whether or not, they would keep the house, if everything else went. When Renne talked about pounds and dollars and francs and marks, there was one picture. The house was her spirit—she had never so loved any house. It was parallel and modern and ran level with lines of mountain, it was squares to be bisected and parallelograms and rhomboids. In the sparse and geometric contour of the house, there was all wisdom. She wanted to walk along the corridors, just that; she wanted to walk from one end of the flat roof to the other far end. She would be so embodied in long parallelograms and in square and cube and rectangle. She wanted those things.

"It wasn't because of last night?" "No, no, it was very lovely. I told you all that. I'm a little upset. Renne would talk so about the crisis. Panic. I'm afraid I've caught her panic." Nat didn't care about Renne and the crisis, but David let her go now. Tenderness drew her back, so that he was satisfied when she kissed him, "good-night."

But Renne and Neil and their money and her money might go. She didn't, now, much care; nothing much mattered, after the psychic loss and shattering, wrought by Neil and his break. Neil turned against her, turned even against Renne. Because somehow he got it into his head that Natalia and his sister were "plotting". It was Renne who found out, but Nat took it all so much as a joke that she blundered in and said, "it's such a joke, Renne really thinks that seventh son of a seventh son thing *has* something in it," as a joke. She said it, as a joke, not really realizing that he and Renne were stricken, that Renne had tried to laugh it off, that family tradition, as "old pre-war rubbish," and Neil had immediately jumped to the conclusion that since "it" had skipped the second of the "other Saundersons" that it would "get" him.

"It" was something vaguely mixed up with a great grand-mother and suicides by drowning, Renne explained it, and "it" getting one of the seventh or one of the seventh of the seventh or one of the seventh being immune against "it." It was all, as Renne said, so much "pre-war rot" but Neil didn't think so, and as, contrary to expectation, the cousin whom he loved, half-mad Kathleen Saunderson, suddenly went "sane," married a Canadian banker and wrote, as far as she was concerned the "charm" was broken, Neil, through a sudden convergence of events, said, "it," having, unexpectedly skipped Kathleen, would get him.

But it wasn't just "it," but a cacophany of events and things. "It" came on him, after he broke with Nat.

A husband might be this or this or this. Neil had never been any of these things. He had been her lover and Renne had really brought them together. Renne was Natalia's half-lover but frightened, "I don't really satisfy you," and at a sort of psychological débâcle of a moment, flung Neil at her. Natalia hadn't wanted a husband but as Renne put it, "now that I'm going north this summer, you better let Neil look after you, as I can't." Neil was a sort of incarnation of Renne, so easy to learn, to know; half of the tenderness, left out in Renne, had been expended on Neil, so that the half-woman made for strength, in the beginning, and the beauty was like May in Provence. Well, Natalia had never been to Provence but the beauty of Neil's eyes was like that; she said, "Neil, yes, I'll come with you, south."

They split the difference, divided the world between them, Renne north, on that impossible cargo boat, in sou'wester and overalls, Neil in his grey lounge suits and colours, south, with Natalia. Capri, that season.

Now he had gone back. She wondered, lying with her wings folded across her back, if he remembered —Capri.

NIGHT X

David sensed something of this, she slept quietly alone now. He was gone now, David was David of the beginning, inchoate, blundering, but with a strain of pure ore, magic somewhere in him. She let him go, watched him, lumbering, centaur or negro about the garden, trying ropes here, helping the Norridge with the refractory frigidaire, interviewing the gas man. Renne handed these things over to David, was busy on a scenario for Una. Una wrote Renne, "you must stay with me in Paris, if your scenario is worth considering." Una was blazing away in the distance, luring Renne out to happiness. David was inchoate, hiding his sudden hurt.

Yet David understood this, though she didn't speak to him of Neil and the post-card, come just now unexpectedly, which said, "I am on my way back." The card was the eternal Faraglioni, and

Natalia wished Neil hadn't sent it. It was possible even now, to fall back, to fall forward onto ice splinters, to be vanquished. She must lie awake, watching parallelogram of bared light, get this clear. If Neil came back—if Neil came back and David— she couldn't think this out, there was no formula to explain it. There was Neil, not wanting her, not wanting David, introverted and sadistic, turned against them, facing his doom. It was childish, but she supposed "nordic." Renne explained it by saying that he really had loved Kathleen. It was possible, the shock of Kathleen's marriage had really meant more than they thought. He had, Renne explained with her modern jargon, "identified" himself with Kathleen. Well—Kathleen!

If the two of them had had a mother, it might have been "mother" (in Renne's jargon) "fixation." Kathleen, an older cousin, would do. Neil appar- ently wanted an excuse anyway, to flaunt off.

If Neil would "stay put," it would be all right, but he would come back. He would slide in and out of doors, and his odd length would add some sort of Omar Khayyam quality to baggy pyjamas, his torse would rise, so ivory, so frail yet so ivory-tower strong, out of the loose baggy trousers of his pyjama suit and his shout for "shaving water, the dam tap's gone again" would be a sharp command, they would all involuntarily drop what they were doing, only not Renne. Thank God for Renne, inoculated against her brother, steady and cynical where they all failed. They turned to him like sun-flowers to the sun, he demanded their attention, their worship, adulation, then when their seared hearts were open to his glamour, he hurled grey hail at them. He demanded their worship and then rained hail, instead of sun-beams.

She would never have known the extent of his provocativeness, if it hadn't been for David. And her terribly proud heart would never have unfurled to David if it hadn't been for Neil. David alone on the roof—that night.

She had to creep in to David, thinking this all out. She had to leave her own bed, having already said "good-night," creep to him, get away from the ice fallacy of Neil. Neil and that damned post-card and his damned charm, so that he had only to send a card, after weeks of neglect, not even saying "I love you" or making some tender comment, but just "I'm on my way back." She could twist it to mean any-thing. It might mean "I'm through with this phase, find this promiscuity after all, a bore," or it might just mean "I'm picking up clothes, books, then off again." It might mean anything, "David."

"Darling." "I'm cold." "That's all right, I'll warm you." "You're such a furnace—how do you manage such magnetic heat?" "It's—just me." She was gone, but not lost, not healed by his vibration. "You're not annoyed?" "How could I be?" "Or—worried?" "O—no." She began to shake, she felt she had got some sort of psychic ague, she was a fool. One card, one damned card and Neil was in the corridor, he was shouting for hot water, cursing the inadequacy of the hot-water system that Renne had insisted on having installed, cursing them all; all but Renne, terrified and waiting for sunlight where hail fell. "David." "Darling?" "What do you remember, what do you remember most, when you're remembering?" He said, quite unemotionally, "I think that first night on the roof, the first night I found you." She was lying still, now. She said, "I never told you. I never told you how near I was." He waited. She said, "it was a miracle. It was only a miracle. I was looking at the stars. There was the square of Pegasus. I got hypnotised and forgot Neil, looking at stars. I was in a sort of funnel. I didn't know how near I was—" The ledge of the roof was low, the flat roof of the house was geometric, modern but the flat ledge was low. The roof was low, three sides, the fourth dropped down; there was the heap of rocks and the slight precipice that sloped down toward the little river. Rocks and jagged edges had never been smoothed down (a place for a mountain garden) and she had seen the geometric square of Pegasus and wings had been fastened to her back. She had known that to leap upward would serve to disorient her, so that she stood for a moment in a black funnel, undecided whether to leap upward—or down on— to those stars. Stars were reflected under her feet— "but it was the door that opened." David asked, "what door?" Then understood, "I had to come out." He had opened the door, the light from the tower-stair shone on her face. He had said, "you want to be alone?" And she had said to a stranger, "yes, David, I want to be alone." Then she had trembled, this same sort of psychic ague, and said, "Neil." She told him of Neil. She had told him of Neil under the Great Square of Pegasus . . . Now she said, "you were drawn, like a feather, to me, in a vacuum."

NIGHT XI

Her heart had been shut like a tight ruby-bud, unfurled. It opened wings or fins, breathed back layers of fins on wings, like a sea-anemone. Her humanity had been shattered, like broken glass, with Neil. To say "Neil" or think of his charm was to stiffen; that heart shut in, cut itself in shutting, became gem to his insufferable precision. "I wish he hadn't written."

The arms tightened, by an imperceptible tremor, then tightened like an octopus. The arms tightened like a cobra, she was caught in the arms, they would break her; if they broke her, it would be only broken bones, things that would crackle and crack and slither, like that tray of cocktail glasses. If he tightened now, by one fraction of a millimetre, the bones would crack and they would be bleached bones as dry as sand, brittle like glass; the heart alone would slither out of that aridity, leap back to its element. "Sadist."

He was there, he was himself, there was no break in any continuity, he did not even know what was going on in her head, he did not know that the crunching of her bones was the highest ecstasy, she would quiver involuntarily away, her stupid humanity would save bones from breaking and the heart that was about to leap, sea-anemone, back to its element, would shut in now, be stable. "You almost broke my ribs."

He said, "sorry," in the British idiom, let himself slacken. He said, "sorry," as a man might, stepping on your toe in a crowded Piccadilly bus, turning round Hyde Park Corner for Victoria. He made Victoria, Hyde Park and Tottenham Court Road blaze out like posters in the underground, or like those mediocre Catherine Wheels that pour pink fire out of bottles, into lighted tumblers, above Piccadilly Circus. A heart, that was somewhere away from her, yet shut in, smothered under lungs and ribs, would compromise. It became pleasant, half-opened; plant rather than sea world, garden-rose in a garden.

"I'm glad you're trying to finish up that article, getting back to your work. I feel you're happier since you've got back to work." She spoke pleasant words, elder sister, protective, wanting him to get on with

his life, pleasant interlude this, Neil Saunderson is, after all, my husband.

Then:

"Do you realise, do you realise what all this is? You do realise the miracle? You do know. I never felt like this, or supposed that I ever could feel. You draw me so near. I don't know what happens. Then, I am millions of miles away, I seem never to have known you, I don't even know who you are."

Then:

"I know. You have given so much. It must be rather frightening for you to give like that, not to know what you give it to. You don't even know what you're giving it to. It requires a terrific lot of courage. You don't know me."

"Why is all this? I wish I had known you when you were eighteen—"

"No. No. Don't ask me to explain why. But if I were eighteen, I would be a person, you would be a person. We aren't now, people."

The darkness drew up, around her. She was safe, here. He was safe, but it was not fair to take him so far, let him drift out so far, then lie in the darkness with the leaves of fern-like trees making a new pattern. There was exigency of new pattern and she knew that the shelf, under the great, square, half-open window was lined with red shells, and bits

of jagged coral and some unfamiliar, unnamed sea-shells. There was no break in continuity, there was a matted hut and dark wooden figures and she and the figures and the shells and the leaves of the fern-like trees were one; they made a unit, there was no break. If she could unfasten her arms, she might explain this.

But:

"*I understand now what it's like to be a cobra. I feel like this; bliss. To wind, to unwind, to lie hours and hours and hours, knotting, unknotting, to wait hours and hours, then twist, to knot, or unknot.*"

"*Yes. Back and back. If I began to talk now, I would chatter like a bird, or make sibilant water-noises like a snake. I might sit up, now, in bed and talk some language—island—Polynesia—India—*"

The darkness falls out of some other-hemisphere, they lie entwined, sea seeping; its aura fills them, leaf to tree. There is no localization of their force. It creeps into bones, dissolves personality, so that they lie, sex undifferentiated yet, through some magnetic law, one receives, one gives. She lies negative to his positive, dim ray.

NIGHT XII

"A house," she says flippantly, "a house, a house, a house." But it is not this house she is thinking of; she is restless, broken, she is incarnate, no red-shell on the window shelf, no blank square of Pegasus, but a greyish sky outside; she is incarnate, suddenly restless, peevish; he says, "don't you like my room, now?"

She says, "yes, it's been almost too much. Sometimes, when I sink down like that, I am almost—lost. I didn't want a body, I didn't want to be a person. To-night, I feel some old human atavism, I feel, I want to wave a hand, say to a dozen minions, keep the corridors quiet, keep lamps burning; I want to walk across thick carpets, open a door in a wall, pour out rose or pearl or white liqueur in cups, talk half the night in a loud voice—" she is whispering, repeats, "*a loud voice*," and her sense of restriction is acute; hearing the Norridge for the second time,

click on the electricity at the far end of the hall, she is enervated suddenly, there is the long progression, really, of these whisperings, the suppression in expression that is getting into consciousness. He said, "I suppose it's because Neil sent that wire."

She said, "no," and went again limp; now, she knew it was not because of Neil and the wire; something was drawing to an end, that was all. The great billow that had lifted her out of her stagnant misery, had broken, flung her high on the dry sand, then curving about her feet, it kissed her, curved into her body, impregnated her with all the sea. The sea of life was there in reality, she was part of that great rhythm. She had not been lost. A billow had detached itself, from all the ocean, for one moment, impersonated "David."

He must not know that she was troubled really. She was not really troubled. She could go on now. She could just go on now. Neil would come back, but the torse, rising from the fern-patterns of those special pyjama trousers, would just be the rather thin but firm body of a modern young man, a body that was made to move, to step, to climb, to dance, maybe. It would be, "Neil Saunderson, my husband, we are very fond of one another, you know, modern, live—well, semi-detached lives these days." Neil Saunderson.

The name was the name of a middle-ageing young man. He was not so young, really. It was this year and not next year that would decide him. "I expect he's been very happy in the south." She felt the arms, those arms; she was drawn back by the wave. David said, "and you, Neith?"

He called her Neith now, and she was flung on a shore that had no end, no beginning; all time converged from that shore, that river. She wanted to be incarnate, mediocre, her ideas were cheap, she wanted to feel that she would put a hand out and pull a brocade gown toward her and she wanted slippers of some soft fur, mink, maybe; she wanted a certain kind of slippers to pad across the floor in. "The bed is too small."

"Why didn't you tell me—I could have come to your room." "O, it's not that. It's that feverish Norridge. Those women—she's got a cold or something." The Norridge had blighted the night. He said, "I can't let you go. You could go. I would let you, if I felt you were quiet, were going to be quiet, sleep." He kissed her, but her nerves jangled; a dog let out an obscure yap under the window. Cars made the usual rumble, but sparser these cold nights; there was the blur of the stream—the stream—"listen." She heard him say, "listen," and said, "it's that damned Norridge."

He said, "is poor Norridge stronger than we are? Why do you let her blight—this?" He would drag her down; she would perceive fronds of fern, but that was the pattern on Neil's pyjamas; she would perceive pattern of unfamiliar sub-tropic bush and trees, but her mind zigzagged off, went triangular course like a dragon-fly on the surface of stagnant water. She was hovering over a stagnant pond, while the sea was waiting, while it had only to draw her—out—

NIGHTS *has been set in Monotype Goudy Modern*
and printed letterpress, from the type,
at A. Colish, Inc. in Mount Vernon, New York.
It was designed by Bert Clarke.